Cosmic
BANDITOS

A. C. WEISBECKER

Cosmic BANDITOS

A CONTRABANDISTA'S QUEST FOR THE MEANING OF LIFE

 NEW AMERICAN LIBRARY

New American Library
Published by New American Library, a division of
Penguin Group (USA) Inc., 375 Hudson Street,
New York, New York 10014, USA
Penguin Group (Canada), 90 Eglinton Avenue East, Suite 700, Toronto,
Ontario M4P 2Y3, Canada (a division of Pearson Penguin Canada Inc.)
Penguin Books Ltd., 80 Strand, London WC2R 0RL, England
Penguin Ireland, 25 St. Stephen's Green, Dublin 2,
Ireland (a division of Penguin Books Ltd.)
Penguin Group (Australia), 250 Camberwell Road, Camberwell, Victoria 3124,
Australia (a division of Pearson Australia Group Pty. Ltd.)
Penguin Books India Pvt. Ltd., 11 Community Centre, Panchsheel Park,
New Delhi - 110 017, India
Penguin Group (NZ), 67 Apollo Drive, Rosedale, North Shore 0632,
New Zealand (a division of Pearson New Zealand Ltd.)
Penguin Books (South Africa) (Pty.) Ltd., 24 Sturdee Avenue,
Rosebank, Johannesburg 2196, South Africa

Penguin Books Ltd., Registered Offices:
80 Strand, London WC2R 0RL, England

Published by New American Library, a division of Penguin Group (USA) Inc.

First New American Library Printing, March 2001
20   19   18   17   16

Copyright © Alan Weisbecker, 1986, 2001
All rights reserved

 REGISTERED TRADEMARK—MARCA REGISTRADA

LIBRARY OF CONGRESS CATALOGING-IN-PUBLICATION DATA:
Weisbecker, A. C. (Alan C.)
Cosmic banditos : a contrabandista's quest for the meaning of life / A. C. Weisbecker.
p.   cm.
ISBN 978-0-451-20306-9 (alk. paper)
1. Drug traffic—Fiction.   2. California, Northern—Fiction.   3. Quantum theory—
Fiction.   4. Colombia—Fiction.   5. Physics—Fiction.   6. Dogs—Fiction   I. Title.
PS3573.E3979 C67 2001
813'.54—dc21   00-051112

Printed in the United States of America

PUBLISHER'S NOTE
This is a work of fiction. Names, characters, places, and incidents either are the products of
the author's imagination or are used fictitiously, and any resemblance to actual persons,
living or dead, business establishments, events, or locales is entirely coincidental.

The publisher does not have any control over and does not assume any responsibility for
author or third-party Web sites or their content.

God does not play dice with the universe.

—Albert Einstein

Not only does God play dice with the universe,
but sometimes he throws them where they
cannot be seen.

—Stephen Hawking

Foreword to the New Edition

An odd occurrence, even by my standards.*

Picture it this way: You've offed your home, a comfy if rustic little villa with a wood stove and deer standing outside the picture window. You've summarily given up a movie and TV writing career that's been quite good to you over the years, although it currently appears to be going nowhere.** You've sold, chucked or given away everything that might impede swift, economical movement and hit the road—it's just your dog and you, with no plans to return.

You've burned bridges.

Your former life seems over, *kaput*. The only apparent

---

meaning to your new life is based on this idea: You're in search of an old friend and sometime partner in crime who vanished into the wilds of Central America five years before. You have little idea of what you're going to say to this guy if and when you track him down—although you do have some questions in mind—or where you might go and what you might do afterward, but that's the plan.

In some sense, what you're doing is an attempt at making sense of things, of your life.*

Truth is, you're about halfway out of your mind.**

You're in far southern Mexico now, four months into your bolt. You left in 1996 but it's now 1997. You've pulled over onto the side of a road labeled *Mex* 200 on the map. You cut your engine. There's no traffic. It's very quiet. You're staring at a sign indicating a turnoff to a town some distance inland. Motozintla. You're suddenly feeling dizzy and a little disoriented—a little *more* disoriented than usual. You've seen this word, this name, before.

Where?

Had a ring to it when you first saw it.

You say it aloud. Motozintla. Moe-toe-ZEEN-tlah.

Still has a ring to it.

In your mind you travel back in time to 1982. Your life of crime is over, recently abandoned due to ridiculous, though dangerous, circumstances. You're staring at the first page of a composition book. You start writing. Your goal is to make sense of things, of your life.†

Before that first session of writing is finished, you find you've turned back to the first page and printed at the top the

---

*You will fail miserably, of course.

**A related issue: You are currently trying to get the reader used to the excessive footnoting to come.

†You will fail miserably, of course, but in this case with a certain panache.

words *Cosmic Banditos*. You don't know where this came from, since you have no real idea of where the story is going. You're completely winging it. About all you've accomplished so far is the description of a dog. You shrug and press on.

Back on the roadside in Mexico in 1997, you dimly recall that at some point in the writing you did back in 1982, you needed a town in southern Mexico for some things to happen in. You'd pulled out a world atlas and searched for a name that has a ring to it. Motozintla. The characters in the story you're writing have an adventure in Motozintla, then move on.

So: You're staring at a sign indicating the turnoff to a place you've written about as if you'd been there, but of course had not. You'd made everything up, including your physical description of Motozintla.*

But that's not why you're feeling weird.

You're feeling weird because you're beset by a creeping epiphany.

The term déjà vu comes to mind, but it isn't quite accurate.

How about *vújà de?* An experience you're sure you've never had before but gives you the willies anyway, because you may have *imagined* having it.

You glance at your dog, sitting beside you in the cab of your pickup truck, looking at you in the way dogs do that asks the question, What's next?

Normally, the sight of your dog has a calming effect on you, but now the reverse is the case. For the moment, your dog's presence is no help at all.

---

*In your writing, you have an overall cavalier attitude toward geographical veracity. You've given Bolivia a coastline, for example, because you needed a South American country name that starts with a *B*, to alliterate with the words *bandito* and *burrito*, yet has a coastline. Bolivia, of course, is landlocked.

Your dog is a big part of your creeping epiphany, your *vújà de* experience.

In order to avoid eye contact with your dog, you look out the window, only to find yourself again staring at the Motozintla sign, which sports an arrow pointing off toward the right, to the turnoff. Your sense of dizziness, of increased disorientation, of heightened weirdness, increases further.

What's going on here?

This: The tale you wrote in 1982 in order to make sense of things appears to be actually taking place now, fifteen years later. By the way: Although the tale was inspired by real events in your life, the crux of it was not only made-up, but essentially nonsensical.*

Yet here you are.

The hero of your fictional tale is in the throes of a crisis. His former life appears to be over, *kaput*, due to ridiculous though dangerous circumstances, and he's about halfway out of his mind. Spurred to action by rising dementia, he embarks on a quest with his dog through Mexico and Central America, in search of an enigmatic figure who presumably has the answers to some important questions. En route, he comes across various banditos, fugitives, corrupt establishmentarians, and all-around lunatics and miscreants.

You, while on this real-life quest to find your vanished old chum—an enigmatic figure for whom you have some questions—have encountered various banditos, fugitives, corrupt establishmentarians, and all-around lunatics and miscreants.

The hero of your fictional tale has a peculiar obsession, having to do with the physics of matter and energy.

You have a peculiar obsession, in practice quite different from that of your fictional hero, but—come to think of it—

---

*The phrase *complete crock of shit* comes to mind.

with identical theoretical roots: the physics of matter and energy.

One of the essential themes of your fictional tale is the idea that human beings exist in different *branches of reality*, an unaccountable number of them, and all of them are real. In other words, *anything that can happen will happen or may have already happened.*

This realization causes you to swallow with an audible gulp.

You look at your dog, who is brown with asymmetrical white patches here and there. Her ears are out of alignment and she has a large tongue that always hangs out, giving her a clownish appearance.

This is the exact description of your fictional* hero's canine sidekick. *A clownish appearance*—these are in fact the words you used in that first writing session to sum up the fictional dog's appearance. The thought crosses your mind that your real dog** was born in 1987, five years *after* you'd described the *other dog.* Further, you teamed up with this current dog accidentally. You did not pick her out of the canine multitudes due to a predilection for brown dogs with asymmetrical white patches here and there, ears out of alignment and large tongues that always hang out. Dogs with *clownish appearances.*

In fact, none of what's taking place can be explained by your innate predilections, storytelling preferences or some sort of interconnection between the two. And anyway, remember: The real events are taking place fifteen years after the events you made up.

The word *coincidence* pops into your mind, then pops right back out again. You thumb through your mental thesaurus but

---

*Given the implications of the *different branches of reality* concept, the usual definition of the word *fictional* should henceforth (and, as a matter of fact, retroactively) be viewed as suspect.

**Better phrasing might be *the dog sitting beside you in this branch of reality.*

don't come up with anything that accurately defines the situation.*

You're still staring at the Motozintla sign. Thinking maybe you should make the turn, follow the arrow** and pay Motozintla a visit. See who, or what, shows up there—or is *already* there.

Or maybe not. Maybe you shouldn't go anywhere near the place.

Out of the corner of your eye, you dimly perceive that the dog sitting beside you is still looking at you with that expression that asks, What's next?

Okay. So much for this Motozintla business.

It was now midsummer of 1998, going on two years since I'd bolted south to find my old friend. Lots of stuff had happened—a ridiculous amount of stuff. Geographically at least, I was back where I'd started in the United States. I was a better guy, if a sadder and wiser one, as a result of dealing with all the stuff that happened. I was no longer about halfway out of my mind. More like a quarter, maybe less. Say, eighteen percent.

I contacted an old stateside buddy, just to say hi and to inform him that I was still among the living. At some point, he mentioned that the fictional tale I'd written in 1982, and which had been published as a book in 1986 (and almost immediately gone out of print), was causing a stir on the World Wide Web.

In dealing with all the stuff that happened over all those months since the Motozintla creeping epiphany, *vújà de* experience, bizarre twist of fate, whatever, I'd pretty much forgotten about my old book, *Cosmic Banditos.*

---

*The phrase *twist of fate* does come close, especially if you add the adjective *bizarre* to the front.
**The phrase *arrow of time* occurs to you.

Listen: While I was gone, while I was *away*, I'd been mostly in very remote places. Places at the ends of various roads and beyond the ends of those roads. In the bush. I'd been essentially incommunicado with the civilized world. Being a low-tech kind of guy to begin with, in 1996 I was only vaguely aware of the World Wide Web. By 1998, if anything, I was even less aware of it, having forgotten what little I'd previously known. I'd hardly seen a TV set in the last two years, never mind this newfangled communications network.

My friend told me to check out *Cosmic Banditos* on Amazon.com.

My initial reaction to this was to wonder why a wilderness outfitter would see fit to mention this book I'd written years ago.

Eventually I got around to learning a bit about the World Wide Web, and yes, the book was causing a bit of a stir. Aside from a bunch of ridiculously enthusiastic reader reviews on Amazon.com, discussion groups had been started; one fellow ran a *Cosmic Banditos* Web site; another had published the first four chapters on *his* Web site, under a banner announcing that *Cosmic Banditos* is the best novel ever written; the book was featured on several recommended reading lists, including one that specialized in *philosophical*(!)* works. There was my name, alongside the likes of Carl Jung, Carlos Castaneda, Immanuel Kant, Hermann Hesse and William Shakespeare. My book and I were at the top of another list, which specialized in Science Fiction and Fantasy.** A German rock group had dubbed itself the Cosmic Banditos. I even stumbled upon a Web site that had swiped the image of the fictional dog from the book's

---

*Once again, the phrase *complete crock of shit* comes to mind.
**The fact that *Cosmic Banditos* is neither Science Fiction *nor* Fantasy would seem to be in keeping with all this.

back cover for use as a logo, and that used the word *bandito* in its E-addresses. The term *Banditomania* kept cropping up. And so on.

The other thing I noticed was that people were clamoring to get copies, which were apparently very scarce. Expanding my World Wide Web search, I was astonished to discover that my little trade paperback was now selling for up to $300 (for copies in good condition and apparently signed by me), at rare-book stores and at auction. (The original cover price was $5.95. Ahh . . . the good old days.)

I was amused to find that I was often referred to as "the enigmatic author."*

I called a rare-book store in Santa Monica, California, and made inquiries about my old book, meanwhile failing to mention that I was the enigmatic author.** The fellow I spoke to offered to sell me a copy for $150. He said the reason for the low price was the copy's condition. A previous owner had apparently made lots of notes in the margins. This piqued my curiosity, but not to the tune of a hundred and a half.

Warming to the subject, the fellow then informed me that he'd recently come across some interesting information via a reliable source in the rare-book biz. He paused for dramatic effect.

"The author, this guy Weisbecker, doesn't actually exist," he said.

---

*I know: A lot of *enigmatic* characters already and we're still only in the Foreword.

**One reason for this enigmatic business has to do with the About the Author note I penned at the end of the tale, and which I've left intact for this New Edition. You may wish to glance at it now. (Don't peek at the last paragraph of the text; you'll ruin everything.) Back? Okay. I was trying to place myself on this side of the fine line that separates *mysterious* authors from *unknown* ones. *Enigmatic* was exactly what I was going for: I'd finally succeeded at something.

Were it not for the fact that I make the assertion that this Foreword to the New Edition is written at least in the *spirit* of nonfiction, I might have here claimed to have been beset by another creeping epiphany, or maybe to have been astrally projected back to the roadside near Motozintla, Mexico, in 1997. I might even have come up with another goofball term, like *vuja de*, to describe whatever inner experience I would be alleging. In point of fact, my reaction to the above theory regarding my nonexistence was much more mundane and predictable: I was swept up in an almost overwhelming sense of scholarly superiority.

"Word is," the fellow at the rare-book store smugly rambled on, unaware of my overwhelming scholarly superiority, "that Thomas Pynchon* actually wrote *Cosmic Banditos.*"

I was given momentary pause as I reflected that there *was* a connection between Pynchon and myself. A connection that the fellow on the phone might find interesting, if he thought about it. The connection was this: Pynchon and I shared the same literary agent. This could be viewed as a potentially suspicious, even sinister, circumstance, especially if one is given to belief in conspiracy theories regarding authors who don't actually exist.** I was tempted to point out the three-way relationship between Pynchon, myself and the agent, just to get the fellow's reaction, but then realized that there was a conceptual problem in doing this. I needed to simultaneously maintain the original theory, i.e., that the author of the book, this guy Weisbecker, me, doesn't exist, for the three-way relationship revelation to be meaningful. In other words, if the theory of my nonexistence went out the window—was, in effect, defenes-

---

*Still *another* enigmatic figure.
**Also: No one has ever seen Pynchon and me in the same room together. Just trust me on this.

trated*—by my owning up to being me, then the three-way relationship would be neither suspicious nor sinister.** In which
case, why had I brought it up at all?

This is exactly the sort of paradoxical conundrum that
makes time travel an unlikely scenario, at least in our branch of
reality.†

Over the months since my return from Central America, I've
been in contact with some of the folks who have been causing
a stir about my old book. To my surprise, the vast majority have
been smart, funny, very cool people. Predictably, however,
some out-of-whack and even severely unbalanced individuals
have managed to surface. Here's a tiny excerpt from a mammoth, politically bent, *Cosmic Banditos*–related tome I received
via E-mail (this comes somewhere near the middle):

> The way to get rid of class struggle is not to think of every-
> thing in those terms, and to devise a utopia that will put an
> end to it from within the particular consciousness from
> which it was conceived. This is the basic attitude problem of
> the Marxist banditos (in the book) and the reason they don't
> get along with their Cosmic colleagues. "They don't even
> like dogs" (an observation by the book's narrator) is yet an-
> other example of something very important. They are ideo-
> logically incapable of liking dogs because in their minds
> dogs are not participating in a class struggle.

---

*I've been waiting a long time for the opportunity to use this word.
**It wouldn't even be a *coincidence*, or a *twist of fate*, bizarre or otherwise.
†If you're not following all this—or, come to think of it, if you're annoyed by
all the footnotes—I suggest you put this book down and forget about it—and
me. It's just not going to work out between us. If you're quick in getting back
to the bookstore, maybe you can get your money back, or at least effect an
exchange—for some sort of self-help book, possibly. (If you bought this book
via mail order, say, through Amazon.com or—especially—through my Web
site, the phrase *you're out of luck* comes to mind.)

The probability that the story conveyed in *Cosmic Banditos* would actually happen is probably very small; but it is not impossible. *Cosmic Banditos* might be an improbable story but not an improbable one (sic).* It is a humoristic work, with psychedelic ingredients. But it is also a philosophical work about human knowledge and the perception of reality. You could call it a postmodern pulp "tzeuberg."

And so forth.

I feel no shame in admitting that the "postmodern pulp 'tzeuberg' " bit left me in the dust.

Just one more example of this sort of thing, but one with potentially distressing implications. In 1991 I bought 100 copies of *Cosmic Banditos* from its original publisher, Random House, at a much reduced price. Something like a buck a piece. This was possible because the book hadn't yet caught on** and Random House was desperate to dump the stacks of it that were cluttering up its warehouse.

I'd love to be able to claim that I bought the 100 copies because I suspected that my book was on the verge of rising from the ashes of the remainder bin to become a cult phenom, and that I could then make a killing (100 books at $300 a pop—you do the math), but (again, in the spirit of nonfiction, etc.) alas, such was not the case.

The Gulf War had just started and my plan was to send the 100 books, in separate mailings, to "Any Soldier" over there. (The U.S. government supplied an address for this sort of thing.) This was to be my way of supporting our troops†—the troops themselves, not the hypocritical, greed-driven slugs who had sent them off to war. I'd written a note on the title page of

---

* Actually, I like this sentence very much.
**It was *lying dormant.*
†Also: The *randomness* of the plan appealed to me.

each copy, requesting that the book be passed along to a comrade when the soldier was finished reading it. I stamped my mailing address under the notes, sat back and waited to see what would happen.

The results were spectacular.

Over the next few months I received *stacks* of letters from our Gulf War troops—more than 100, all told—proof that the troops had done as I asked: The book had been widely circulated.*

This came as a shock, but what took me even further aback was the fact that no one said anything negative about the book. I was in fact prepared for some severe hostility from folks who are in theory the very epitome of the establishment mind-set. You see, aside from being a nonsensical complete crock of shit, the tale I wrote in 1982—in order to make sense of things, of my life—is riddled with drug usage, rampant criminality, blatant and unapologetic nihilism, and all-around chaos and destruction.**

But apart from some gentle chastisement from a few devout Christian types, the reactions were uniformly positive. Possibly a nonsensical complete crock of shit riddled with drug usage, rampant criminality, blatant and unapologetic nihilism, and all-around chaos and destruction is exactly what human beings who are waging war need, to put their situation in its proper perspective.

One letter stood out, however, as an example of something. Around 20 pages, handwritten in a minuscule scrawl, it made the Marxist/bandito manifesto excerpted above look like

---

*Just how widely is an important question, to which I will return. *Anon.*

**Someone once asked me if there were any books to which I might compare *Cosmic Banditos*. Groping for an intelligent response, I finally came up with this: "It's sort of like that Russian novel, *Crime and Punishment*, except there's no punishment."

an archetype of brevity, style and clear thinking.* My initial thought was that the author was some poor, disoriented grunt who had slipped through a crack in the system and been accepted into the armed forces by unfortunate accident.

Not so. Based on the return address at the end, the guy was an officer, a captain and a military lifer. Interpreting the implications of some of his gibberish, it became evident that he was in command of a bunch—a veritable *shitload*—of Patriot missiles.** My tale of drug-ridden random chaos and destruction had apparently struck a deep chord in the fellow's psyche.

From the day I received the letter until the troops came home, I watched CNN's coverage of the conflict with some trepidation, fearing that if something untoward happened with a shitload of Patriot missiles, I would have been somehow responsible. Listen: *I'm not kidding.*

Indeed, on several levels, the episode is a perfect example of something.

One more thought about this Gulf War business and how it may be directly affecting *your* life, at this very moment. The thought goes back to how widely the book had been circulated among the troops. My theory is that it had been *very* widely circulated. How else to explain my receiving more reactions than the number of books I'd sent? And, obviously: Not everyone who read it would have taken the time to respond. In fact, given that the folks over there were somewhat busy dodging bullets and artillery fire, ducking Scud missile barrages,† avoiding poison gas attacks, yelling at reporters to get out of the way

---

*I'd love to run an excerpt but in stripping down my life preparatory to my Central America bolt in '96, I accidentally threw out the box containing my Gulf War fan mail, having gotten it mixed up with my financial records.
**The other thing that became evident was this: The author, this guy Weisbecker, me, was perceived as a godlike figure. I had apparently *figured it all out.*
†And, in retaliation, dementedly, perhaps randomly, firing off shitloads of Patriot missiles.

so they could return fire—all the neat stuff that goes with waging modern war—it's likely that only a very small percentage of
people who read the book contacted me.

What if *thousands* of Gulf War troops had been subjected to
my nonsensical crock? And what if my nonsensical crock had,
for a high percentage of those troops, put their situation in its
proper perspective? In other words, had a positive effect, essentially perverse though it may have been? And then, those
troops having come home, what might they have told their
friends and loved ones about this book they'd received out of
the blue? And what might have then happened, in terms of demand for the book?

Do you see what I'm getting at?

The timing would have been right. As far as I can figure, in
1991 *Cosmic Banditos* had not yet begun its rise to pop cultdom.
People were not yet clamoring for copies. Proof of this is the
fact that Random House had gleefully coughed up a bunch for
a buck a throw.

Yet, soon enough, people would be clamoring for copies.

Paying hundreds of dollars for copies signed by the author.*

The direct upshot being that the powers-that-be in the
publishing business would see fit to give *Cosmic Banditos* another
shot.**

What we have here is a convoluted, ridiculous chain of
cause and effect, for the moment terminating with you reading
these words.

By the way: As you will likely soon find out, convoluted,

---

*At the risk of repeating the obvious: Somehow, simultaneously with my sig-
nature being of monetary value, the rumor would circulate that I don't actually exist.
**A somewhat *tentative* shot, based on the actually existing author's nonexist-
ent advance.

ridiculous chains of cause and effect are what the fucking book is *about*.

Speaking further of what the book is about, any or all of the following concepts may be occurring to you at this moment: creeping epiphany, arrow of time, bizarre twist of fate, enigmatic, *vújà de*, Motozintla, Bolivian burrito (or Bolivian bandito), clownish, postmodern pulp "tzeuberg," you're out of luck, *kaput*.

And, need I say it? A complete crock of . . .

This book is dedicated to people who stick together*

---

*Which, come to think of it, is what it's *really* about.

Traveling back in time to 1979 . . .

✴ 1 ✴

Exiled

I am very poor right now.

Yesterday I had José bring me a box of Milk Bone Flavor Snacks for Small Dogs. My dog—High Pockets is his name— weighs well over a hundred pounds. I didn't want to worry him unduly, so I had José borrow a handful of Milk Bone Flavor Snacks for Large Dogs from one of his cousins in town who has a large dog (a stroke of luck since Milk Bone Flavor Snacks of any size are difficult to get in Colombia).

I got High Pockets into a Canine Feeding Frenzy with the Flavor Snacks for Large Dogs, then started slipping him Flavor Snacks for Small Dogs.

If High Pockets noticed that his Flavor Snacks diminished in size, he kept it to himself, but every time I look at that god-damn Pekinese or whatever it is looking out at me from the box, I get depressed.

High Pockets has taken our drastic change in lifestyle in relative stride. He is easily lifted from depression by a pat on the head, a kind word or even one of the above-mentioned

Milk Bone Flavor Snacks for Small Dogs. He has displayed amazing resilience and compassion. He probably saw our downhill slide into financial oblivion coming and prepared himself for it. His optimistic Worldview is a constant source of comfort to me in these troubled times. I suspect that none of High Pockets' ancestors had much in the way of doggy possessions, and this may account, at least in part, for his devil-may-care attitude about money. He also doesn't have an affluent *look* to him. He is quite sizable, as I have mentioned, and has the largest tongue of any known mammal. It always hangs out (even when he's sleeping) and his ears are out of alignment, giving him a clownish appearance. His hair is medium in length (as is mine) and is sort of a reddish-brown with asymmetrical white patches here and there (my hair, by the way, is dark brown). All in all, High Pockets represents a wild night of crap-shooting at the Canine Gene Pool.

Occasionally I enjoy lying on my bathroom floor listening to my primitive toilet leak. High Pockets is always there with me, his Flavor Snack breath and wet nose providing a certain perspective, a sense of serenity, that would otherwise be lacking. The sound of running water, the companionship of a Contented Canine Soul and the comforting feel of damp linoleum frequently send my mind reeling into the most delightful of reveries.

When we are not on the bathroom floor, High Pockets and I like to stretch out on the thistle- and rock-strewn front yard and listen to my sad little radio play the one station that reaches this far into the Sierra Nevadas de Santa Marta. Sometimes I turn the radio off and we don't listen to anything.

The other day High Pockets and I decided to do some work on the shack, what with the rainy season only three months away and all, so I had José bring us up a hammer and some nails. We dismantled what was left of the porch and used the lumber to patch the roof. Then I went out back, set up some cans and bottles and shot them with my M-16.

As usual, Legs showed up soon after target practice, slithered his way up the M-16 and wrapped himself around the barrel for his afternoon siesta. Legs is a small boa constrictor who lives under the shack. He likes the warmth of the barrel after a few hundred rounds have been shot through it. If I've been shooting the 9mm José gave me for my birthday, he'll wrap himself around that. After about a month, Legs had it wired as to which gun I'd been shooting and would go right to it without having to sniff around with his little pink tongue like he had to do at first. Snakes are supposed to be deaf, but I guess Legs gets vibes from the air or something. Anyway, he can tell the difference between a 9mm and an M-16. I know that for a fact.

High Pockets doesn't care much for Legs and Legs doesn't care much for High Pockets, but they've reached an understanding of sorts. High Pockets has agreed not to harass Legs and Legs has agreed not to bite High Pockets on the nose and make little tiny holes that leak blood.

Problems occasionally arise at night. Sometimes Legs gets in late from a night of crawling around in the jungle. If he's had a bad night, if he's lonely or whatever, he likes to come up and sleep in the bed with me, especially if there's a nip in the air. High Pockets sleeps with me also.

Legs is a feisty little guy and High Pockets doesn't like to be awakened from whatever weird dreams dogs have, so late-night confrontations occur maybe once a week. I've noticed that Wednesdays are popular, though I have no conception of why this should be the case. I consulted José about it, and he promised to check with some local dude who knows an Indian who knows a lot about snakes and their Worldview, but the Indian has been on some kind of crazed fast and won't talk to José's buddy about snakes or anything else.

Since we have no electricity up here, the nights are a little dismal, but we have oil lamps and a small kerosene stove. Sometimes José comes up and we play cards or dominoes while High Pockets watches. On these special occasions José and I usually get very fucked up on drugs and alcohol and pass out.

One night José brought up some of his cronies and we all had a great time—except for High Pockets, who had the runs and spent most of the night outside squatting on the lawn.

José says that in a couple of months, when things cool down a bit, High Pockets and I will be able to go into town once in a while and shoot some pool and get drunk with him and his Bandito Buddies.

José and I have a lot in common. We're both in our midthirties (José *looks* a bit older) and we're natural leaders. I am a little taller than José and José is a little heftier than me, but he definitely isn't fat. He's as strong as the proverbial bull and just as quick to anger. Our recent problems have cemented our already close friendship into a fraternal bond. José and I are, in short, blood brothers. Spiritual brothers. *Bandito Brothers.* I trust José with my life every day, he being the only human who knows my whereabouts. He brings his Bandito Cronies up only when they're too drunk to remember how they got here. If I never have another friend, I shall consider myself fortunate to have known José. High Pockets feels the same way, and his taste is impeccable.

José and a couple of his cohorts went into Santa Marta last week (a long trip by donkey and Land Rover) and mugged a family of American tourists at the airport. Amongst their spoils were a camera and several books. José gave them to me, which was very nice of him. So I've taken up photography (he didn't get any film, but I'm working on my composition nonetheless) and reading. José also gave me an assortment of their personal effects including unmailed postcards (he had peeled off the stamps) that were apparently written on the doomed travelers' flight from Aruba. Having little else to do, I took a somewhat Sherlock Holmesian interest in these artifacts of José's victims.

According to bits and pieces of ID, they're a family of four from Sausalito, California. A father, a mother and two teen-age daughters. One of the daughters—Tina is her name—had written her boyfriend, Tom, informing him that Aruba is nice and that she hopes they will be able to get together when she gets back. She then claimed that she loves him and added about a thousand little X's all over the card, almost obscuring the address (also in Sausalito).

To tell you the truth, I think Tina is full of shit. The tramp had also written to some guy in San Francisco—Gary is *his* name—and dropped a few innuendos that led me to believe that old Gary is going to see some serious action when Tina returns home. She also claimed that she loves *him* and did her little X's routine again. For my own amusement I counted the X's on both cards. Tom got the nod as far as numbers was concerned, but Gary's were neater and more symmetrically arranged. I am contemplating dropping both of these assholes a note to let them know their situation as far as this little slut is concerned. I spoke to José about it at some length, and he thinks I should do it—adding that if he'd known about the situation at the time of the mugging, he would've knifed Tina on the spot. José was so pissed off that he threatened to go back to Santa Marta in order to avenge Tom and Gary's masculinity, but I doubt that he'll go through with it.

The other daughter, Ruth, wrote about twenty postcards, none of which are worth going into. As a matter of fact, Ruth's correspondence depressed me. She wrote mostly to relatives and girlfriends, and from her choice of pictures on the fronts of the cards I suspect that Ruth is a troubled young person. José

confirmed my suspicions that she is overweight and intro-
verted. He claimed that while the rest of the family was
screaming and trying to escape, Ruth just stood there looking
down at the ground. José mentioned that even in the heat of
the moment he felt a twinge of sympathy for this morose and
chronically lethargic young girl.

The mother's name is Kimberly and she wrote only one
card, to her doctor. She assured him that her infection had
cleared up, then signed off.

The father either didn't write any postcards at all or else
managed to mail them at the airport before José and the boys
descended upon them.

Their diverse personal effects didn't offer much to go on
except to confirm my suspicions about Tina. The underage
nymphomaniac had brought her diaphragm along on the trip.
I knew it was hers because it was carefully concealed in the
lining of a makeup case with her initials on it. Apparently the
little pig didn't want some customs official whipping it out in
front of her parents. She was obviously prepared to sexually
terrorize the population of whatever country her parents
turned her loose in. I will not fail to mention this fact to Tom
and Gary in my forthcoming notes.

I don't intend to say anything about the concealed diaphragm to José, however. He has a very short fuse and, when
he is agitated, his behavior is unpredictable.

Amongst the family's reading material was a current issue
of *Seventeen* magazine—Tina's, no doubt. I read it cover to
cover and was completely disgusted by nearly every article. I
haven't spent much time in the States lately (for reasons I will
go into presently, I may never go back), and I had no conception of how far downhill the moral fiber of America's
young people had slid in my absence. As an exile, I feel I have
a certain perspective that gives me the right to make a moral

judgment on this matter. Based on *Seventeen*, I have come to
the conclusion that America's pubescent females have completely run amok.

After reading the goddamn thing, however, my attitude
toward Tina softened somewhat. She is obviously under incredible social pressure to subject her barely developed genitalia to
copulatory or self-inflicted stimulation as often as possible.

I made the mistake of translating one of the articles for
José. He went berserk, scaring the shit out of High Pockets,
who bounded out the door and disappeared into the jungle.

The rest of the reading material obviously belonged to the
father, unless Tina counts Subatomic Particle Physics and Cosmology amongst her other, mostly biological, interests. I suspect that her knowledge of nuclear physics consists of no more
than idle gossip about the Big Bang Theory.

The titles of these books are enough to give a person of av-
erage intelligence the intellectual shakes, but I've been plowing
through them anyway, having little else to do. At night, after a
hearty dinner, I turn up the kerosene lamp and read to High
Pockets while the wild animals grunt and hoot outside our little house. This is heady stuff, especially if one's been isolated in
the jungle for a long while with a dog, a snake and unlimited
drugs. For example:

> The many worlds interpretation of quantum mechanics says
> that different editions of us live in many different worlds si-
> multaneously, an unaccountable number of them, and all of
> them are real.

I read this paragraph a few times to High Pockets, put the
book down, smoked a joint, had a few shots of homemade rum,
then reread it to myself.

Until I got to this passage I wasn't taking the book very seriously. I thought it was a complete crock of shit, as a matter of fact, but this concept, I must say, gave me pause.

. . . different *editions* of us live in many different worlds . . . and all of them are real.

Holy shit, I thought to myself in a flash of insight. I lit another joint, exhaled contemplatively. "What do you suspect he means by 'editions?' " I asked High Pockets.

High Pockets whined, as he always does when I address him directly, but I wasn't sure what he meant. He sneezed a few times.

José rode his little burro, Pepe, up from the village the next day with food, ammunition and drugs. He could see I was upset. I sat him down and attempted to explain the problems I was having with the idea of different editions of us living in different worlds simultaneously. He listened, nodding his head sagely, then told me not to worry. He had a buddy who knew an Indian who was familiar with these matters. It turned out to be the same guy who knew the same Indian who was on the fast and wouldn't talk about snakes, so I'm not holding my breath.

If there are any other editions of High Pockets and me out there, we would like to hear how you guys are doing. The editions of High Pockets and me that are sitting in a shack in the wilds of South America aren't doing real terrific. As I mentioned at the outset, High Pockets and I are financially destitute. This is especially upsetting (to me, anyway—as I explained, High Pockets is unconcerned with financial matters) since just a few months ago we were worth several million dollars.

High Pockets and I also have serious legal problems. We're being actively pursued by every law enforcement agency in the Western Hemisphere (and probably by every *edition* of every agency, if agencies have editions like the rest of us). This is why we are living in the shack. We are, as they say, keeping a low profile.

José is taking care of us, financing our seclusion, as it were, because we are old friends and partners in crime. José is a Full-Blown Bandito and, according to the Bandito Code of Conduct, must look after his down-and-out cohorts.

José is a stand-up guy, and times have been tough for him, too, as they seem to be everywhere. He felt really bad about our having to subject High Pockets to the ignominy of consuming Milk Bone Flavor Snacks for Small Dogs, but as I told him, the small ones last longer and they're not High Pockets' main staple anyhow. High Pockets eats the same food I do, and I don't get any between-meal Flavor Snacks of any size or description, for chrissakes.

How High Pockets and I reached our present space-time coordinates (that book again) and came to the violent attention of the authorities is a convoluted and sad tale.

The reason I am relating this at all is the same reason I have for studying Cosmology and Quantum Mechanics: There is little else to do.

> Not only is the Universe stranger than we
> think—it is stranger than we can think.
> —Werner Heisenberg

Operation *Don Juan*

At least the weather was good, but it *always* was. Eighty-two degrees, fifteen- to twenty-knot Northeast Trades, a few cumulus clouds that never passed in front of the sun. It was Antigua, British West Indies, and it was one of those days. Sort of. Robert and Jim, my friends and shipmates, were sitting with me at the Admiral's Inn, English Harbor, working on our third bottle of Mount Gay rum and trying to figure out what had gone wrong on our last voyage to Colombia. A voyage that resulted in the loss of our boat and some 10,000 pounds of marijuana. Cap, a local who occasionally worked for us, sat down and helped himself to a belt of rum.

I adjusted my sunglasses and watched Loopie rowing out to *Trick*, the eighty-foot trimaran that had just set an unofficial transatlantic speed record with a crew of drunken Swedish lunatics. The new record stands, but no one on the boat had sobered up long enough to find out what island they'd collided with. They'd been aiming for Barbados, several hundred miles to the south.

I remembered Loopie's aborted career as a fellow Contra-bandista several years back. We were still in the harbor when he cracked his head with the main halyard winch handle as he raised the sail, trying to wave to his girlfriend at the same time. "Oh, mon, oh, mon," he said before losing consciousness. He didn't look fit for an extended voyage, so we dumped him on the fuel dock, set the spinnaker and pointed the sloop in the general direction of the 8,000 pounds of gold buds that José and the boys had handpicked in the mountains just south of Santa Marta. High Pockets was only a few months old at the time and, being a natural sea dog, came along for the ride.

The trip was successful, with only a handful of minor disasters. High Pockets has been an enthusiastic Canine Contra-bandista ever since.

Robert was glaring at Jim balefully, his face and eyeballs bright red. Jim is a wiry Texan with a very sick sense of humor. He's a lot smaller than Robert, and their bizarre, antisocial antics prompted their nicknames (all serious Contrabandistas have nicknames): The "Comedy Team from Hell" or, when they're not together, "Mutt from Hell" and "Jeff from Hell."

I was sure Robert was going to do one of his numbers. He did. He picked up our table and heaved it into the shallow water next to the patio. It was an impressive throw. Rum bottles, glasses and money drifted slowly toward the mangroves. Various seabirds and bartenders squawked in fright and protest.

I got up and headed off the owner of the Inn before he could get near Robert.

I spread some E.C. (Eastern Caribbean) bucks around and procured another table and a couple more bottles. Robert was smiling at Cap when I sat down again. Jim was howling, razzing Robert about his boils. The ones on his ass. Beating across the Caribbean into twenty-knot head winds for weeks while sleeping, eating and living on wet marijuana bales tends to upset one's normal complexion, especially on one's posterior. Robert's eyes glazed dangerously as Jim yelled to a table of nervous tourists that Robert had the biggest, grodiest boils in the islands. The most artistically arranged as well.

"Drop trou' and show 'em, sport," Jim said.

Now *I* was getting nervous. There was no point in trying to shut Jim up. He was drunk and rolling, and loved it when Robert ran amok. Plus we had just lost close to two million dollars, along with our boat, so nobody was in a good mood.

"He's gonna blow," Jim said. "I'm calling for a seven point five on the Robert Richter Scale."

Cap sensed he was in trouble. He smiled artificially at Robert, and Robert continued to smile back. It looked like someone had painted his contact lenses red.

"Oh, mon . . . Shit, mon." Cap was now very frightened. To me: "Wot I do now, mon?"

Robert liked Cap. Cap had helped us get the *Wayward Wind* ready for her last run. Cap was a stand-up guy. Cap was a family man. Cap liked animals. Unfortunately, Cap was about to experience grievous bodily harm. Jim was grinning sadistically.

I had to distract Robert. If he would just look at me for a few seconds, Cap could maybe make good an escape.

"Hey, Robert, remember the old *Don Juan?*" My voice was casual.

Robert, Jim and I had first met on the *Don Juan* a couple years earlier in Panama. She was a rusted-out 180-foot freighter whose real name escapes me. We dubbed her the *Don Juan* because of the frequency of sexual activity experienced aboard during the two months we spent refitting her for an attempt to break the known record for weight of marijuana carried in one vessel. We were all associated with the same international crime cartel and hit it off quickly. We were ensconced in the Holiday Inn in

Panama City. This was during the time of the Senate investiga-
tions of the Panama Canal treaties. We'd had two Congressmen
evicted from their rooms so our contingent could control the
whole twelfth floor. Including High Pockets, there were thir-
teen or fourteen of us, depending on who had use of the Lear
that day.

We had already burnt out the Hotel El Panama, mostly due
to Robert's rampages, some of which, I must say, were justified.
I would've thrown that whore off the balcony myself, under the
circumstances.

There were several conflicting theories circulating as to
just who the fuck we were. We cultivated some of them in sub-
tle ways. It was obvious that we were on an incredible expense
account (incredible being one step above unlimited). We paid
cash for everything. We looked like criminals. And we were
completely disorganized.

To the Panamanians all this meant we were U.S. government people, probably CIA. Which meant they didn't want to
offend us during the treaty talks, which was okay with us.

There were other rumors, but the CIA one was my personal favorite, and also the most popular. A casual remark to a
cabdriver, a cryptic P.O. box in Guatemala as my registered
address, a dinner with a Congressman who was told by someone (probably the desk clerk, whom I bribed constantly) that
I *was* CIA . . . it all added up to our being Washington trouble-
shooters.

Robert was feared by everyone in the hotel. Word had
leaked from the El Panama: If real trouble broke out (and it almost did), Robert was rumored to be a one-man CIA Death
Squad. No one at the Holiday Inn said a word when Robert put
all the cabs outside the main door on retainer ($10 an hour)
and ordered them not to move unless he told them to. And
none of them did. So for nearly a week, no one could get a cab

at the Holiday Inn. No Senators, no Congressmen, nobody. They had to hire private cars at great expense to the American taxpayer, while Robert played with his taxi fleet.

He'd come out the door in his straw hat, Aloha shirt and plaid slacks—all 240 pounds of him—and whistle. Twenty cabbies would be at attention in front of their vehicles in maybe four seconds. That's fast for those latitudes. "Gentlemen, start your engines." Robert was into auto racing. He would give each man a piece of paper with an address on it, always the same address on each piece of paper. At Robert's signal, they'd all take off to fetch whatever it was he wanted—drugs, booze, a whore or all three. A hundred dollars U.S. for the man who returned with the goods. He had twenty crazed Panamanians roaring through the streets of the city in his own private Grand Prix.

Back in Antigua, one of Robert's eyes blinked. I interpreted this as an indication that some primitive thought process had started up in his brain, that maybe a synapse or two had fired in some kind of normal sequence. Even Jim was startled. Cap was frozen to his seat, still riveted by Robert's red-eyed zombie grin.

"He blinked," Jim said.

"I saw," I said.

"Wot dat mean?" Cap said.

"I don't know," Jim said.

"He's coming around," I said.

"Wot he gonna do when he come 'round?" Cap said.

"I don't know," I said.

"I think he liked it when you reminded him of the Grand Prix of Panama City," Jim said.

I never met a Contrabandista who didn't love to sit down with one of his kind and reminisce. It sometimes seemed like that was half the reason for doing something weird. You could talk about it later.

Even in Robert's prerampage catatonia, these fond memories were having an effect on him. How they would alter his subsequent behavior was anybody's guess. It was a crapshoot, no doubt about it. I pressed on. Why not? I was starting to enjoy myself.

The *Don Juan* was a tribute to Murphy's Law. In fact, the ship went so far beyond Murphy's Law that a new law had to be formulated. *Don Juan's* Law: "Anything that can go wrong already has, and will be that way forever."

I was the captain, but I swear I had nothing to do with choosing her for this run. I have a simple method of surveying big steel ships for structural flaws. I take a 12-pound sledgehammer down into the bilge and start swinging. Whatever breaks is not structurally sound. I immediately started a leak in the forward-most chain locker. A few more swings took out her corroded watertight bulkhead.

That was when Julio appeared, wide-eyed and yelling in Spanish. I have a pretty good command of the language, but all I could make out was *"gringo loco."*

Julio was the engineer of the *Don Juan* and had been since his father died twenty years before. This accounted for many of his peculiarities, such as an obsessive crossing of himself, the dozens of crucifixes he had hanging all over the engine room, and an irrational fear of silence. Much later, in a relatively calm moment, Julio explained this last one. Most of the moving parts on the *Don Juan* would freeze up from time to time for various reasons. Julio would somehow unfreeze them. He had this recurring nightmare that every moving part of the ship would freeze up simultaneously, leaving nothing but *"silencio, hombre, silencio completamente."*

Anyway, after my initial inspection of the *Don Juan* and her engineer, I attempted to reason with the multinational syndicate that was financing the operation. I remember the conference very clearly. I was supposed to confer with the Colombian onloading crew as to timetables, code names, latitudes and longitudes, radio frequencies, and various contingency plans. The conference had obviously been in full swing for at least three days. The first thing High Pockets and I noticed was the Colombian Dope Lord, Eduardo "El Gordo," stark naked and passed out across the twelve-foot conference table. He was drooling into a pile of cocaine, a tendril of which led across the table and over the edge. About a quarter pound was scattered on the shag rug. I sensed that the reason everyone was unconscious was the dozen or so mostly empty bottles of pharmaceutical quaaludes that were scattered among incalculable magnums of Dom Perignon. ('69, by the way. You could still get it in those days.)

Altogether there were six or seven Colombians (including José) and maybe eight or nine of my gringo associates (including Jim and Robert) in various states of naked repose, along with several whores, including, incredible as it sounds, the one Robert had thrown off the second floor balcony at the El Panama. Except for a cast on her left ankle, she looked fine. Under the conference table I found an unconscious room service waiter, naked except for his red Holiday Inn vest.

Looking back on it now, this may seem somewhat humorous, but at the time I was horrified. I had to *reason* with these people. My life, and a shitload of money, depended on that ship. However, under the tutelage of Robert and Jim, my professionalism went, as they say, by the boards. Within a week High Pockets and I were attending the regularly scheduled (or continuously running) "conferences." I was—and I'm not bragging here—responsible for as much drug consumption and damage to the premises as anyone else except for Robert, who managed to convert two singles into a suite while High Pockets chased the hotel security guards around the circular twelfth floor and out the fire exit.

I did slur out a few complaints about the ship, so Eduardo ordered $100,000 to be spent on improvements. Money, I was told, was no object when it came to the "sheep," as Eduardo called the *Don Juan*. The only problem was that the ship broker spent it all on sophisticated electronic navigational gear instead of new plates and welds for the hull. I remember snorting a huge line of flake and yelling, "Great! We'll know exactly where we're sinking!" The sick thing is that I was genuinely enthusiastic about this concept.

Four or five days of drug-ridden, sex-crazed dissipation and vandalism was about all my system could handle, so High Pockets and I packed up our gear and headed for the checkout desk. I felt morally obligated to spend some time aboard the *Don Juan*. We attempted our escape at three in the afternoon, figuring our associates would be comatose by then, but Robert and Jim staggered in the front door just as we were checking out. They were on the tail end of a major league drug binge. Robert's right eye looked like the Black Hole of Calcutta; his left was swollen shut with a rainbow shiner. He collared me and dragged me to a couch, accusing me openly of being a lightweight and a disappointment to the twelfth floor.

I made the mistake of trying to be logical. The ship needed attention, was my line of reasoning. I tried to explain the structural weaknesses that my aborted survey had revealed.

Robert countered my logic by dropping a gram or so of coke on the lobby table. "Anybody got a straw or something?"

Jim rolled up a fifty dollar bill and handed it to him. Robert snorted half the pile, rocks and all, then handed me the bill. I glanced around the lobby to see if anyone who wasn't on our payroll was lurking around. Just a few tourists and Congressmen. I had a healthy snort, grabbed my bag and bolted before Robert could react.

"I'll be on the ship!" was my exit line.

The *Don Juan* appeared deserted, but I found Julio kneeling in the engine room in front of the rusty old diesel, saying a Hail Mary.

After he forgave me for the sledgehammer incident we got along quite well.

Julio was obsessed with the *Don Juan*. She had had six or seven owners in the past twenty years, and Julio had stayed on through them all, for reasons known only to himself. He spent at least fifteen hours a day tearing apart machinery, jury-rigging, crossing himself and trying to reason with the ship. Julio was strange, no question about that, but I didn't realize how strange until I got a look at his cabin.

Most sailors have pinups over their bunks and Julio was no exception, except that his were full-color fold-out diagrams of new diesel engines, generators and spare parts. He knew that ship, though—he really did. As the skipper I was happy to have him along, weird as he was. I bought him some welding equipment so he could repair the damage I'd done with the sledge. I never went into the bilge again, for fear I'd put my foot through the hull and sink us at the dock.

Julio was an extremely valuable asset in another way. High Pockets and I had started frequenting tourist bars. I'd wear an old captain's hat, horizontally striped T-shirt, a three-day growth and an unlit stogie. We'd track down tourist chicks or military brats who were looking for "atmosphere" and drag them back to the *Don Juan*, improvising hair-raising sea stories on the way. If the *Don Juan* had anything, it was atmosphere. Julio played the Walter Brennan role, holding down the fort. He'd pretend he was drunk, I'd yell at him for being a rummy, he'd yell about dead bees in Spanish, then I'd corner the chick in my cabin. She'd look at High Pockets with his big pink tongue hanging out, then at the cracked and peeling paint, the dirty mattress, then at me, with my cigar, captain's hat and bottle of cheap rum. It was Bogart and Bacall as far as she was concerned. Once I got 'em aboard the old *Don Juan*, it was all over but the moaning.

I could've gone on this way forever, but late one night Robert and Jim showed up. It was a nightmare.

The sun was starting its descent over English Harbor when Robert began to growl. Softly, from deep down in his chest. At first Jim and I thought it was distant thunder. We looked around for cumulonimbi, but there were none.

"It him, it him, mon." Cap was sweating profusely now. I had almost forgotten about him. I motioned for another bottle of Mount Gay. High Pockets let loose another sneeze.

"Say what, Cap?"

"It him. He be growlin'."

"Who? High Pockets?"

"Shit, mon. Robert. He be lookin' at me and he be growlin'. Like las' time."

Cap had seen Robert run amok once before, at a local bar called the Spinning Wheel on the other side of the island. Apparently Robert had done some growling there, too. The Spinning Wheel was now being rebuilt under new management.

"I remember," Jim said, referring to that night in Panama. "Robert was fucked up. Jesus, was he fucked up."

Robert's growl deepened further, as if he were trying to speak.

"Mebbe," Cap said, "I just be gettin' up slowly an' be goin' on my way."

"I wouldn't recommend that," I said.

"We'd hit every bar and whorehouse in Panama City," Jim said. "Then Robert gets it into his head that we had to pay you a visit. See if you needed anything. Drugs or whatnot."

"Where'd you dredge up those two chicks?" I said.

Robert's growl increased in volume. Cap began to tremble.

"What chicks?" Jim said.

High Pockets and I were fast asleep in our cabin with a little honey we'd run into in town when I heard this horrendous bellow, then a splash. I jumped up in shock, thinking the *Don Juan* had busted a gut and was on her way down. Then I heard Jim laugh. Two frightened females were whispering. Another incoherent bellow, this one mixed with water. I stuck my head out the porthole and looked straight down. Robert was trying to heave his huge body out of the water and back onto the wharf via a slippery old warp. Jim was looking down from the edge, howling. He had a magnum of Dom in one hand and a magnum of .357 in the other. A huge joint was sticking out of his mouth and the bottom of his face was coated with a fine mist of Peruvian flake.

A few yards away, two overweight girls were huddled in fear.

"What is it, hon?" inquired the little Cupcake on my moth-eaten mattress.

"Nothing," I lied. "Nothing." I sensed that there was going to be trouble. Maybe serious trouble. "Put down the gun, Jim." I was trying to be calm, but we were in the Canal Zone, which at the time was still controlled by the American military. With tensions between the U.S. and Panama as strained as they were, I had the sickening feeling that a shot fired here could start a revolution or a soccer match.

Jim put the pistol to the end of the joint and drawled, "I reckon I'll just shoot it lit."

"No, wait, Jim," I stammered. "Uh-uh."

He lowered the gun. "Wha?"

"Uh, ain't you gonna introduce me to your lovely lady friends?"

"Wha?"

Robert emitted some inhuman sounds and then, with a bovine roar, managed to haul himself onto the wharf.

"Put the gun down, Jim," I said.

"Who are you talking to?" asked my little Plum Crumpet.

"Nobody," I said. "Nobody."

Robert had gotten to his feet. He pulled a water-soaked glasine bag from his plaid polyester jacket.

"Goddammit! Cocksucker! Piss cunt ratshit!" echoed around the Canal Zone.

I could hear Spanish voices from the Panamanian side. It sounded like they were taking up defensive positions in response to Robert's gringo battle cry.

"I'm horny," said my little Honey Pot.

Robert threw his ruined bag of coke into the water and demanded some of Jim's. Jim put the .357 magnum to the end of the joint again.

"Just a minute. Lemme fire this sucker up." He cocked the piece.

"Jim!" I yelled. "The ladies! Introduce me, will ya?"

Jim pointed the pistol at one of the girls. He closed one eye, trying to remember. "Lemme see. This is . . . uh, shit." He pointed the piece at the other girl, who let out a small, weird screech.

"And this is . . . uh, the other one."

At this point Robert pulled a hand grenade from his jacket pocket and hooked his middle finger around the pin.

"Gimme the coke or I'll blow myself up," he announced.

"Oh, yeah?" Jim pointed his piece at Robert, waving the barrel a foot under his nose.

"Pull that pin and I'll blow your head off, asshole."

I sprinted out of my cabin and ran into Julio on the lower deck. He was watching Robert and Jim in their Polish standoff. High Pockets staggered out, bleary-eyed.

Seconds passed.

The fat girls whimpered.

Somewhere up the canal, a ship blew its horn.

My little Cheese Danish called out for me to come back to the cabin.

Julio crossed himself.

High Pockets was having one of his sneezing attacks.

The tension mounted.

Then Robert pulled the pin.

There was a faint hissing sound. A little wisp of smoke rose from the top of the grenade.

"Gimme the coke," Robert said.

"All right, just lemme light this baby first," Jim said. He put the magnum to the end of the joint and pulled the trigger. There was a bright flash and a loud bang. The shock and recoil of the weapon sent Jim flying about ten feet backward. He landed on his ass, then looked curiously at the joint. It was still in his mouth, a lot shorter now, and still unlit.

Searchlights were turned on and a siren was wailing nearby. I could hear the sound of running boots on pavement and the gruff voice of somebody deploying troops.

The two overweight girls were screaming uncontrollably.

Robert was looking at the hissing grenade, trying to remember something.

Julio was saying a Hail Mary.

High Pockets was squatting and straining in the throes of a serious defecation.

My little Cranapple Strudel was yelling something from my cabin.

"Robert!" I called down. "Remember that trout fishing trip you told me about?"

Robert looked up at me, or tried to. His eyeballs were moving around independently, like a lizard's.

"*Arrgarah,*" I think is what he said.

"Trout fishing! How do you do it?"

His face lit up in revelation. He tossed the grenade into the Canal.

Baboom! About a ton of water and dead fish rained down on the wharf and the *Don Juan.*

At this point our position was overrun by the Marines.

What followed was the first but by no means the last time that High Pockets, Robert, Jim and I would be interrogated by military and/or law enforcement agencies. The Marines quickly released the two overweight girls and my little Pumpkin Truffle. They had enough on their hands with the four of us plus poor Julio, who rambled on continuously about the heads backing up on the ship from the concussion of the explosion.

I was obviously carrying the ball since Robert and Jim were actively hallucinating. Jim was attempting to catch a bat that was circling his head, while Robert kept trying to dislodge something from his left nostril. As his grunts became more coherent, I realized what his problem was: A pig had somehow become lodged in his nose and Robert had him by one hoof and was attempting to pull the animal out.

The interrogation didn't start right away. The two CID men and three military intelligence officers were staring dumbfounded at Robert and Jim as they struggled with their marauding hallucinations. That was okay with me. I had to decide between several contingency attitudes that had proved successful in similar situations. I opted for reliability rather than creativity.

"Hey, assholes," I said, "do you have any idea what you've done?"

Robert seemed to have the pig halfway out of his nose. It was a big one.

"What?" a distracted CID man asked.

"I said, do you have any idea what you've done?"

"Let's see some ID, fella," said military intelligence officer number one.

"Your friends here, who are they?" asked military intelligence officer number two.

Before I could respond, High Pockets let fly the most horrendous doggy fart I'd ever been subjected to. It was one of those devastating, silent jobs that makes your eyes water.

This hard-assed, crewcutted Marine captain, being the senior officer, took charge of evacuating the room.

"Leave him here," I said, referring to High Pockets. "Let him sit in his own stench."

As usual, High Pockets refused to acknowledge the mindless act he'd perpetrated. As everyone else bolted for the door, he remained seated with that shifty-eyed look he uses when he fucks up.

Anyway, after we relocated and settled down, the interrogation resumed.

"What are you doing in the Canal Zone?" a CID man asked.

"First of all, none of you assholes are cleared for any of this information," I said, "and judging from your handling of this situation, none of you ever will be."

Then I started asking for names, ranks and serial numbers. Crewcut made a few threats, so I made a few threats, so he stood up and made more threats, so I stood up and did likewise. Robert stood up and started beating the shit out of the pig. Jim caught the bat.

"Good work, men," I said.

"What are you doing aboard that ship?" The CID man was trying to calm things down.

"Okay, assholes, have you ever heard of the code name *Don Juan?*" I said.

They all looked at each other, each afraid to be the first to admit ignorance.

"I thought not," I said sarcastically. "That ship out there is the most important advancement in electronic eavesdropping equipment yet developed."

Julio nodded his head for some reason. *"Sí, sí."*.

"Who were you shooting at?" Crewcut asked.

"Left-wing guerrillas," I said. "Security has obviously been breached. We have to move that ship immediately."

"I don't believe a word of this shit." Crewcut again.

Jim was asking one of the CID men if he had any 'ludes. This was going to be close, so I played my trump. To Crewcut: "You ever hear of Congressman Kaminsky?"

He had. This was the Congressman I had cultivated over dinner at the Holiday Inn. By the end of the meal he was completely confused about who I was and what I was up to. I told him that if he ever needed a favor, he should contact me through Langley. I told him to mention Operation *Don Juan.* With politicians, if you offer them a favor, they figure they *already* owe you one.

"He's on the committee that oversees you clandestine military assholes and your appropriations, right?"

"So?" said Crewcut.

"He's here. Over at the Holiday Inn. My operational name is Don Juan One. Call him. Tell him you have me locked up here and see what he says."

A half hour later we were back at the Holiday Inn conference room. I was trying to revive Eduardo. Robert was on the phone with room service attempting to order a magnum of

Dom, but the words weren't coming out right. Jim tried to help, but he sounded like a 78 record played at 45.

I found a straw and blew about a half gram of flake up Eduardo's nostrils. He started coming around. It was vital that we get the *Don Juan* and ourselves out of Panama. There was a lot of bureaucratic confusion, what with the Canal treaties getting close to a Congressional vote and the Panamanians threatening to take the Canal by force, but it was only a matter of time before "Operation *Don Juan*" was discovered to be run by a bunch of drug-crazed anarchists with colorful criminal records. I figured Crewcut had already been on the phone to whatever contact he had at the CIA in Langley. We had one thing going for us: None of the dunderheads at the Agency would care to admit they hadn't heard of *"Don Juan,"* just in case there *was* such an operation. The pettiness of those jerks, their internal power struggles, and their rivalries with other agencies (especially the DEA) made our organization's antics seem downright ingenious. I calculated that we had at least six hours before the awful truth was uncovered.

Eduardo opened his eyes and sat up. He smiled, then his eyes closed as he slowly slumped forward and rolled off his chair onto the floor. I scanned the conference room for signs of life. All the key members of the syndicate, gringo and Latino, were there, but they all appeared to be in deep comas.

"Robert," I said, "try waking up José there."

"Gralpnlop!" Robert yelled into the phone, then slammed it down on José's forehead, missing the receiver cradle by a yard. He looked at me quizzically.

Jim was in the bathroom dry-heaving.

The only thing I could do was leave a note, collect High Pockets, Robert and Jim and beat cheeks back to the *Don Juan*. I'd instructed Julio to fire up the old clunker and be ready to cast off.

I found a piece of paper and printed in large letters: "Eduardo: *Muchas problemas. Tenemos que salir ahora mismo. Te veré en Riohacha en 48 horas.*"

I stuffed it into a half-full jar of quaaludes, where I knew someone would find it, grabbed Jim, then told Robert about the ounce of Peruvian I'd left on the *Don Juan*. We were back on the ship in fifteen minutes.

We cast off and headed north; we would pass through the Canal, then turn east into the blue Caribbean, where, I hoped, we would somehow meet up with Eduardo and the boys. And 100,000 pounds of Guajiran Gold.

"A hundred thousand pounds," Jim repeated softly.

The sun was starting to get low over the hills behind the Admiral's Inn. I thought briefly about Admiral Nelson, whom the inn was named after, about the Battle of Trafalgar, the days of sail.

Someone was strumming a guitar from an anchored yacht.

> *Yes, I am a pirate,*
> *Two hundred years too late.*
> *Cannons don't thunder,*
> *We've nothing to plunder,*
> *I'm an over-forty victim of fate.*
> *Arrivin' too late,*
> *We're arrivin' too late . . .*

I looked at Cap, who seemed on the verge of collapse. Exhaustion, fear, helplessness. There was something primal about his confrontation with Robert. His fate was in the hands of a mindless, indifferent entity much more powerful than himself.

"My leg," Cap said. "It done falled asleep, mon."

I looked at Robert. The warmth from a quart and a half of

rum had spread throughout my body. I was at peace with myself. It appeared, from my angle at least, that Robert had started to glow dimly around his head and shoulders. His mind was reaching critical mass. Yeah, it would soon be the Fourth of July in Robert's skull. There was nothing I could do for Cap, so I waved for more rum and relaxed, waiting for the display.

> *I have been drunk now for over two weeks*
> *I passed out and I rallied*
> *and I sprung a few leaks . . .*

"I don't remember much about the trip to Riohacha," Jim said.

I had lied about the ounce of Peruvian. There was no coke at all aboard the *Don Juan*. Robert didn't take the news very well, but I had planned ahead, as all competent skippers must. I tricked him into going down into the main cargo hold, locked the door, then broke the bad news by yelling through the loading hatch. Robert, of course, went berserk. The remake of *King Kong* comes to mind, when Kong was trapped in the Supertanker.

From on deck I could see Robert, fifteen feet below in the cavernous cargo area, pounding on the hull. I threw Valium-laced bananas and papayas down to him, but they had little effect. Julio was concerned about the integrity of the ship's hull. I was worried about the fact that we were extremely short-handed. Jim had swallowed the rest of the Valiums with a quart of rum and would be out of action for a day or so. We wouldn't pick up the Latino contingent of the crew until we reached Colombia, if we ever did.

We negotiated the Canal without incident, although I had to bribe several Panamanian officials who wanted to know if we had an endangered species of local fauna in the cargo bay. I breathed a sigh of relief when we were off soundings and heading due east, leaving Panama a foggy, twisted memory.

Julio had drastically overestimated the *Don Juan's* cruising speed. I had expected to get at least eight knots out of her, but she maybe made four and was frequently stopped dead in the water by rogue head seas. It was just Julio and me for the first twenty-four hours. He refused to leave the engine room and I couldn't leave the helm. Aside from High Pockets, the only semblance of human company I had was Robert's bellowing from the cargo hold, just for'ard of the bridge. Eventually he stopped, leaving only the sounds of the wind and sea and the rumbling of the tired old diesel far below. I was starting to get drowsy when Jim staggered onto the bridge with a fifth of Mount Gay.

"Jesus Christ, am I hung over," he said. "It feels like this whole fucking place is rocking around."

He hadn't figured out that we were underway.

"I'm out of drugs. Let's cruise on back to the Holiday Inn."

"We're a day out from Panama," I said. "This show is on the road."

"Where's Robert?" Jim wasn't listening.

"I locked him in the 'midships cargo hold," I said.

"Where's the bathroom," Jim said. "I gotta throw up."

"The bathroom? You mean the head?"

Then it hit me. It should've been obvious from little things they'd said in Panama, but I was either too preoccupied or too drugged to pay any attention. Neither Jim nor Robert had ever been at sea before.

Jim walked out onto the bridge wing and scanned the unbroken horizon. He rushed back in.

"All right, wise guy, where's the fucking dock?"

I tried to be casual, but there was an edge to my voice. "Uh, what exactly are your functions on this operation, you and Robert?"

"Robert used to be with the U.S. State Department. He's our liaison to whatever country we're laying waste to. I'm in charge of travel arrangements and pharmaceutical quality control."

"Oh," I said.

"Now where's the fucking dock?"

"About a hundred miles behind us."

"Ohhh . . . shit!"

Jim ran to the bridge wing. "Robert!" he screamed.

Robert tried to answer from the cargo bay but all he could come up with was a loud, drawn-out belch. The acoustics of the empty cargo area gave the sound a stereophonic quality, but Jim zeroed in on its source immediately. He made it to the loading hatch and peered inside wide-eyed. He was genuinely panic-stricken.

"Robert!" he screamed. "We're both gonna die!"

Robert groaned, then uttered his first coherent word in a day and a half. "Good," is what he said.

Shadows were lengthening. The sun had dipped below the hills behind the Inn. Tourists and yachtsmen were filling up the patio and ordering sundowners. A ten-piece steel drum band was setting up. They were all local boys wearing white pants and flowered shirts. Luckily, Robert was still staring at Cap and hadn't noticed. Robert didn't like steel drum music.

Jim stuck a straw in the bottle of rum and put the end in Robert's mouth. The dark brown liquid started to disappear.

"Good boy, yes, yes," Jim said. He was treating Robert like an attack-trained Doberman. This I hadn't seen before, so I inquired about it.

"I just want to see if I could maybe control him a little," Jim said. "Think of the possibilities."

"D-dat b-be one g-good idea, J-Jim." Cap's teeth were chattering, even though the temperature was still around eighty degrees.

Robert bared his teeth and growled softly.

"*Good* boy." Jim started to move the bottle away from Robert. His growl deepened significantly. High Pockets started sneezing again.

"Jesus," Jim said. "Do ya think he'd turn on *me?*" He put the straw back in Robert's mouth.

"It's entirely possible," I said. "Remember what happened when we let him out of the cargo hold?"

Jim blanched slightly. The thought seemed to sober him up a bit. He shuddered. "It was horrible. Trapped on that rust bucket with a rabid, two hundred and forty pound lunatic on the loose. And no drugs to calm my nerves."

"It was mostly show," I said. "Just a lot of bellowing and frothing at the mouth."

It was true. Robert hadn't had any food in about a week and no serious drugs for over a day. He ran out of steam on the aft deck while trying to strangle Julio. The crack on the skull I gave him with a belaying pin helped also.

"You guys shaped up pretty good after you got the drugs out of your systems," I said.

I had put them both on a strict diet of prune juice and rum. Robert took orders quite well when he was just plain shit-faced drunk. He steered the ship well, too. He and Jim both had the uncanny ability to get their own alcohol-induced rolling, pitching and yawing into sync with the ship's.

We raised Riohacha, Colombia, four days after leaving Panama. We were two days later than I had told Eduardo in the note, but I suspected that nobody would notice. As dawn broke, we spotted his forty-eight-foot sportsfisherman adrift just outside the harbor mouth. As we pulled alongside, I saw that my worst fears had been realized. Nothing had changed except that the syndicate was now comatose on a yacht instead of in the Holiday Inn conference room in Panama.

Eduardo was strapped into the big game-fishing chair, his chin resting on his chest and an upside-down bottle of Dom sticking out from the rod-holder. José was hanging precariously over the edge of the tuna tower.

The only piece of equipment on the *Don Juan* that was completely reliable was the horn. It sounded like Godzilla in heat. I gave it three quick blasts. This had no effect whatsoever, so I had Julio board the yacht to see if he could revive anybody. No way.

Robert and Jim wanted to give it a try, but I knew they'd just ransack the craft for drugs. So Julio threw us a line and we towed them into Riohacha harbor.

Riohacha is the only sizable town on La Península de la Guajira. The peninsula itself and Riohacha in particular are completely under the control of bands of semi-organized Banditos, Dope Lords and savage Guajiran Indians. The countryside is wild and lawless. The Bogota government has long since given up on the area, possibly because of the bounty on tax collectors, drug enforcement agents and military officers who try to interfere with the mammoth marijuana trade. Riohacha is reminiscent of Dodge City in the 1880s, except for the fact that Wyatt Earp would be machine-gunned to death two seconds after he hit town.

Open gun battles between rival Dope Lords are commonplace in the streets of Riohacha, along with kidnappings, rapes and rampant traffic violations. Tourism is not exactly booming and there is, as yet, no Club Med. But with a pocketful of pesetas and a reliable high-caliber sidearm, a fun-loving guy can still have a good time. And that's exactly what High Pockets, Robert, Jim and I proceeded to do, since Eduardo and José had misplaced nearly half of our 100,000 pound cargo and had (once they came to) taken off to look for it and shoot up some of their neighbors.

Jim and Robert figured they'd start out where they'd left off in Panama, at least as far as drug consumption was concerned. I was seriously considering abstaining altogether, but I was under intense social pressure, so I finally gave in.

We spent about a week in Riohacha and, according to rumors I heard later, we had a good time. Two of the five bodyguards Eduardo left behind to keep an eye on us were wounded in a barroom shoot-out one night, but I have no recollection of it. Robert was said to be at the bottom of it, so I suspect that it did happen, but neither he nor Jim can remember anything either.

I do dimly recall how the night began. We persuaded Julio to leave the ship and accompany us on our regularly scheduled binge. He told us he'd go, but added that he never drank or took drugs. He was a religious man, a peaceful man, he said. Robert smiled knowingly and nodded, then fitted Julio with a bullet-proof vest, gave him a .45 automatic with two extra clips and took him in tow, promising that we'd keep it mellow if that's what he wanted. Julio seemed dubious at first. Apparently the flak jacket and gun had placed some doubts in his mind about Robert's real motives.

Robert's philosophy of self-defense is unique. He himself never carries a gun. He always has a hand grenade in the pocket of his polyester jacket, however. In case of trouble, he pulls the pin, drops the grenade and "lets the chips fall where they may."

Around midnight, Julio agreed he'd have one drink, a toast

to our future good fortune. Jim prescribed a half gram of coke and a ground-up quaalude and administered it to the boy via his drink while Julio was taking a leak. Julio is about half Robert's size, yet our bodyguards swore he did as much damage to the place as his mentor did.

The last image I have of that night is a very low angle shot. I believe High Pockets and I were under a table. Robert and Julio were in the process of taking on the whole bar. Then either the lights went out or I was hit by flying debris when Robert's grenade went off.

"It was probably the grenade," Jim said.

The sun was under the yardarm; the patio was almost full. Waiters were lighting torches around the perimeter and between tables.

"A hand grenade isn't really that weird a method of self-defense when you have Robert's attitude," Jim said. "He's always severely outnumbered. It's amazing how a violent explosion in a confined area will separate the men from the boys."

A few guys in the steel band started plunking on their awful instruments. Robert reacted immediately. His body stiffened and he leaned forward just a tad. Some kind of mist or steam seemed to have enveloped his head. Cap's eyes moved slowly in their sockets in my direction. I had to look away.

"Six or seven notes of 'Yellow Bird' 'll do it." Even Jim was sounding a little worried now.

I sensed that Jim was right. The last couple years had been difficult for all of us, especially Robert. He had begun to talk about the "good old days" when, in the State Department during the Nixon administration, he had been a hot young lawyer specializing in international law and diplomacy. A former Rhodes Scholar and second-round draft pick of the Denver

Broncos, Robert felt that he may have taken a wrong turn at one of the many Crossroads of Life.

Eduardo showed up on the dock early one morning with a dozen or so bale-laden trucks escorted by an army of Guajiran Indians. Clad in loincloths and human-bone necklaces, they were armed with MAC-10 machine pistols, M-16's and bows and arrows.

Most of Riohacha turned out to watch. At the time the largest bulk of marijuana ever to be on-loaded at the Riohacha public dock, it took about two hours and went without incident, except for the odd knife fight amongst the spectators.

Eduardo provided Julio and me with five deckhands, four Colombians and one Costa Rican.

As I approached Robert and Jim on the dock for goodbyes, Robert said, "I don't like it."

"Neither do I," Jim agreed.

"Whaddaya mean?" I asked.

"You and six greaseballs on this ship." Robert shook his head.

"No big deal," I said.

"Julio's okay, but I don't like the look of the rest of these spics," Jim said. "You might need help keepin' 'em in line."

Robert and Jim looked at each other.

Robert sighed. "I guess we're gonna have to go with him."

"I reckon you're right for once, asshole," Jim said. "You got enough grenades?"

"On the ship," Robert replied. "Drugs?"

Jim grinned. "I had a feeling this might happen. I got a fuckin' major-league pharmacy stashed in the galley."

Robert leaped onto the *Don Juan* and bellowed, "All right, assholes, let's get this show on the road!"

I was genuinely moved. I had grown quite fond of those

loonies. High Pockets and I always operated more or less solo, but this gesture cemented a partnership that would endure incredible ups and downs and prolonged stretches of outright insanity.

Unfortunately for everyone at the Admiral's Inn, the band's first selection was "Yellow Bird." On the third note Robert let out a roar that must've been audible in Guadeloupe. High Pockets, Jim and I had seen it coming and dove for cover. Poor Cap's hat flew off and his chair toppled over backward, depositing him in a shallow drainage canal. Suddenly a grenade appeared in Robert's hand. He pulled the pin with his teeth and lobbed it toward the band. It was a good throw. The grenade clattered around in one drum, bounced into another, rolled around the rim like a roulette ball, then came to rest in the bottom of the instrument.

"Live grenade!" I yelled. The boys in the band were frozen in midnote, staring down at impending doom. Suddenly they scattered: Some jumped a low wall behind the bandstand and hit the dirt, some dove into the harbor and stroked for the mangroves, the rest sprinted for the bar or through the patio, hurdling tables. The crowd of tourists and yachtsmen reacted as one, like a school of fish. First they all started to run in one direction, then another; then they all dove under tables and chairs.

The explosion was in B-flat. All ten drums went more or less straight up, spinning like frisbees and resonating from the blast.

Glasses and bottles were shattered by the concussion and flying hunks of steel drums.

Fortunately the bandstand was slightly raised and everyone was lying flat, so no one was seriously hurt.

High Pockets, Jim and I jumped up in order to assess

Robert's mood. He was sitting down, perusing a dinner menu.

"Robert," I said casually, "why don't we cruise on over to the airport?" I was planning our escape from Antigua.

"Yeah, man," Jim said, "forget about dinner. We'll do up some flake on the way."

"Okay," Robert said calmly. He got up and we strolled through the smoky, debris-filled patio. Dazed patrons were wandering around in shock. I could hear the owner on the phone inside the bar, frantically trying to contact the police.

We ambled casually to our rental car, Robert in the middle, Jim and I making small talk in order to distract him from the destruction, panic and disorder he had caused.

We ran into a major snag once we got to the car. Robert insisted on driving. High Pockets and Jim protested, but Robert's eyes began to glaze over again.

"Okay, sport," Jim said.

We piled in. Robert started the engine. "Gimme the coke," he said.

I had to improvise. "It's at the airport."

The drive from English Harbor to the airport is normally very pleasant. Rolling green hills, sugarcane fields and quaint villages. Robert, however, found a route I was unfamiliar with. At one point we were roaring across an apparently deserted pasture. Robert kept glancing in the rearview mirror and grinning. I looked back. A large Brahma bull was at full bore and closing on us fast. He had a horrendous hard-on and was bellowing—presumably for us to stop for a quickie. Closing my eyes and sliding down in my seat, I felt a severe headache coming on.

The next thing I remember was the accident. Robert plowed us into a lamppost and flipped the car in front of the departing passengers' gate at Antigua International. The front of the airport was deserted, but sirens were approaching from all directions. We crawled out of the car and entered the open-air terminal.

The building was deserted except for the customs and immigration officer, who was asleep at his desk. His phone was ringing and ringing. I had a feeling the call had something to do with us. I threw an E.C. double sawbuck onto the officer's desk, then High Pockets, Jim and I guided Robert out onto the tarmac.

Once again my foresight stood us in good stead. Earlier that day I had told our pilots to have the Lear ready and waiting, as I always did when Robert started drinking before breakfast.

The boys up front sensed urgency in our movements, so they quickly fired up the engines and taxied to the runway, pausing briefly while High Pockets deposited one of his meatloaves on the pavement.

I looked out the window: Two police cars and an army jeep were approaching from the other end of the field.

"Maximum angle of climb, Harry," I called to the pilot, using our euphemism for "Get us the fuck out of here!"

Approximately half our takeoffs were made under this kind of duress. Harry had been a two-time ace in Vietnam and enjoyed flying for us.

Eight minutes later we were leveled off at 46,000 feet. Jim was pouring himself a glass of Dom. Robert was stretched out on the floor, snoring, thank God. High Pockets was up front with the pilots, taking in the view.

I whipped out my dog-eared West Indies chart and crossed off Antigua. I then examined it for islands that we hadn't burnt out. There were still a few left. I picked one more or less at random, gave Harry the coordinates, then sat back. Jim poured me a glass of bubbly. I took a deep swallow and glanced out the window at the blue Caribbean far below. Antigua was rapidly receding behind us. I slid a tape into the VCR, then lit a joint. I exhaled contemplatively, wondering if we had started a downhill slide. We had just lost our last boat, but that was nothing new. We'd had several "last boats" since the voyage of the *Don Juan*. Robert had trashed another base of operations, but he had done that *many* times before. Basically everything was as it should be. We'd have spectacular successes and comical failures. Robert would blow things up and we'd have to leave. This was the natural order of things, so there was really no obvious reason for me to wallow in pessimism.

I have a method of pulling myself out of negativity. It is a very simple concept, a short phrase. I had another sip of champers and said it out loud: "It will be interesting to see what happens next."

> *The worldview of particle physics is a picture of* chaos beneath order.
>
> Gary Zukav

✳ 3 ❋

Subatomic Banditos

.

My life here in the jungle has changed completely since José mugged Tina and her family. I have immersed myself in the netherworld of Quantum Physics. My days are rich and rewarding, my nights filled with wondrous speculation. High Pockets and I spend hours on end in the yard staring up at the night sky whilst being bombarded by Subatomic Particles, those elusive little cosmic rascals.

I have not yet launched myself into the study of cosmology, preferring to let macroscopic reality wait in the wings until I have absorbed, as it were, the Subatomic Realm.

I have never felt as at peace with myself as I do now. I am contemplating starting a correspondence with Tina's father, who is clearly a very enlightened man. The margins of his books are replete with exclamation points and question marks. Some of his question marks are particularly incisive—his skepticism about the book's view of quarks and their behavior, for example. I suspect that Tina's father doesn't believe in quarks at all. It's a moot point at best but I would like to know his reasoning anyway.

José and I discussed the notion of starting a dialogue with Tina's father, but our talk turned into a heated argument. José was completely against it. I deftly changed the subject by asking him *his* opinion about quarks, but he was too agitated to think clearly. For now I've let the matter drop.

Since it turned out that José has no interest in Subatomic Particle Theory, I air my views exclusively to High Pockets, usually late at night after one of our meditative sessions in the front yard. I suspect that this has helped him in transcending his somewhat mundane Canine Worldview.

He has also become more serene. An example: A few nights ago, after I gave a particularly insightful lecture on electron generation, Legs crawled up through his favorite crack in the floor and snaked his way onto the bed. High Pockets was stretched out next to me, wide-awake. He didn't say a word when Legs curled up and passed out right in front of his nose. For a moment it appeared that High Pockets was about to have one of his sneezing fits (a sign of doggy distress, I suspect), but he only sighed, closed his eyes and went to sleep.

Last week José, High Pockets and I went on a tiger hunt. It seems that this particular *tigre*—a jaguar—had been decimating local livestock and was number one on the Bandito Hit Parade. A ten-goat bounty was offered by local farmers. High Pockets quickly picked up the scent and bounded off, howling like a maniac, with José and me in hot pursuit. High Pockets knew he was after a cat, but regretted the whole affair as soon as he caught up with it. Evidently he was unaware that the cat he was chasing was bigger than himself. He took one look at it, then, without hesitation or comment, bolted straight back to the shack where he spent two days in seclusion under my bed. But in any case he had done his work, having treed the tiger.

At this point, José and I had another difference of opinion. I wanted to dispatch the animal quickly with my M-16, but

José had other ideas. I had given him a small antitank rocket launcher for Christmas several years earlier, and he wanted to use it. Rocket launchers, I told him, were unsportsmanlike weapons for hunting, and had a negative impact on the environment in general.

José looked at me as if I'd lost my mind, then proceeded to blow up the tiger, the tree and half the hillside. When he attempted to collect the bounty, however, it became evident that the joke was on him. There was absolutely nothing left of the tiger, and none of the farmers believed his story about blowing it up. He even dragged one of the guys (blindfolded for security reasons) up to my shack so I could verify the kill.

I was still angry with José for his unsporting methods and for his ho-hum view of Subatomic Particles, so I just shrugged and said, *"No sé."*

I didn't see him again until yesterday. High Pockets and I were tending our little garden of tomatoes, opium poppies and marijuana plants when he appeared, looking tired and a trifle guilty. He hadn't been sleeping well, he said, and he had finally come to the conclusion that I'd been right all along about the rocket launcher. He promised that in the future he would use it only against rival Banditos and army vehicles. He also promised to use it, whenever possible, in such a way that its effect on the environment would be minimal.

I then apologized for not supporting him in front of the farmer. We embraced. It was a very touching scene.

I had a big favor to ask, so I sprang it on him as he was wiping a tear from his eye. Timing is everything when asking a Bandito for a favor.

The favor, of course, had to do with Subatomic Particles. It was vital that I get certain other books in order to satisfy my ever-expanding Subatomic Horizons. I had compiled a reading list based on the recommendations of the authors of the books that had come my way via Tina's father.

José and I sat down in the dirt and I explained my plan. Being somewhat esoteric in subject matter, these books were unlikely to be stocked in bookstores or public libraries. So I asked José if he'd knock off the University of Barranquilla Research Library. My plan involved having him shave and dress up like a student, then go in and simply steal the required titles by stuffing them down his pants or whatever.

At this point José interrupted me to say that if he was going to knock off a library, he was going to do it in the prescribed Bandito Fashion. With flair, in other words. He then bragged that he and his buddies would not only get me the books I wanted, but they'd also get me every fucking book in the whole place. It then dawned on me that José probably had never been to a library.

His bravado cooled down somewhat when I told him that it would probably take his entire gang two days to load all the books in the library onto eighteen-wheelers.

José stared at me for a moment, dumbfounded. *"Muchos libros,"* he said softly.

"Sí. Muchos," I replied.

José thought it over for a few seconds, then said he'd get the books I wanted but would still have to do it his way. With guns blazing, I presumed.

I did my best to talk him out of it. He kept nodding his head as I spoke, but I could tell from the faraway look in his eyes that he was mentally gearing up for an all-out armed assault. I changed the subject.

It was crucial that I teach José the Dewey Decimal System of cataloging books. One of his buddies knew how to read, so I told him to bring the guy up later that night to go over the system so they wouldn't fuck up and bring back the wrong books.

The evening didn't go exactly as planned. José did bring the guy who could read, but he also brought his whole crew—twenty Banditos, all heavily armed and all completely drunk. I dimly recall going over the Dewey Decimal System with someone, but for all I know it was with High Pockets.

I woke up this morning with a serious hangover and an empty house. José and his buddies had left sometime during the night. I assume they're heading for the University of Barranquilla Research Library, since my list of books is missing. It will probably take them four or five days to make the round-trip, so I'll have to report on this matter as it develops.

Having little else to do, I reread a chapter that delves insightfully into Bohr's famous Specific-Orbits-Only model of the atom.

I smoked a joint, then began to compose notes to Tina's boyfriends, Tom and Gary. For some reason, I had put off writing them, but now I was in the mood. It was time to get the distasteful job over with.

The notes were identical, of course, except that one was addressed to Tom in Sausalito and the other to Gary in San Francisco.

I explained their situation to them, as far as Tina was concerned, then added a few relevant comments about Man's Place in the Subatomic Universe. I did this in order to put the bombshell I had dropped about Tina in its proper perspective.

Of course it occurred to me that I was fucking around with three people's lives, but this is a responsibility I am prepared to accept.

The only bothersome thing about my notes is that they may come as somewhat of a different kind of surprise than one might think. Getting disorienting, anonymous messages from the wilds of South America may shake these guys up in fundamental, psychological ways. Not to mention Tina. When she realizes how her duplicity was uncovered, she might suffer a complete existential breakdown. What I'm saying is that I might be altering these people's very perception of reality.

Nevertheless, I wrote the notes, addressed and stamped them and fully intend to have José mail them for me when he gets back from pillaging the University of Barranquilla Research Library.

Whilst waiting for José, I will continue with the story of High Pockets and me, and how we came to be where we are.

I will next describe the voyage of the *Don Juan*, since some of you out there may be curious about it, even though it's somewhat of a digression. I think it important at this point* to put this tale in its proper temporal perspective. The voyage of the *Don Juan* took place some three years ago. Robert blew up the Admiral's Inn on Antigua about six months ago. I realize that I left High Pockets, Robert, Jim and myself in our Learjet somewhere over the Caribbean, and in a sense we are still up there, waiting for me to continue that part of the story, which I will do when I feel like it.

Can Nature possibly be so absurd as it seemed to us in these atomic experiments?
—Werner Heisenberg

---

*By the way, the expression "point in time" that has become so popular is a redundancy. Since reality is a space-time continuum, the word *point* also takes care of the concept of "time."

❊ 4 ❊

The Voyage of the *Don Juan*

The voyage of the *Don Juan* went smoothly for about three hours. Then Robert started terrorizing the Latino members of the crew, except for Julio, for whom he felt some affection since the night they took on Riohacha together, although Julio denies ever having left the ship. The first thing Robert did was to put a knife to the Colombian cook's throat and explain how he liked his food prepared. He then started making rounds of the ship while juggling three hand grenades.

To prevent a mutiny, Robert made it clear to the "greaseballs" that if he ever caught more than two of them together, he'd blow up the ship and everyone on it.

This kind of talk naturally made the crew a bit edgy, except for High Pockets, Jim and me. We'd long been stoic about the possibility of a Robert-induced sudden death.

Our mechanical problems started about four hours out. The big electrical generator, hooked up to a GM-671, broke its coupling and nearly decapitated Julio with flying parts.

Over the next few hours Julio, who I suspect had some kind of unnatural and possibly perverse relationship with the machinery on the ship, began acting more and more unbalanced.

Soon after the generator packed up, the steering quadrant jammed with the helm hard to starboard, causing the ship to describe huge circles and roll horrendously. As soon as that was put right, the fresh-water cooling pump for the big diesel malfunctioned and pumped all our freshwater into the bilge. Luckily we had plenty of rum and several hundred cases of Heineken for drinking and showers.

Around dawn of the second day the backup generator seized for no apparent reason, leaving us with no electrical power except for a small, gas-driven Honda generator, which we used to keep the batteries charged. By this time Julio had developed a nervous tic in his face and had started sipping rum on the sly.

Just before lunch of that same day, a propane leak caused an explosion that destroyed half the galley, and Jim's drug stash along with it. Naturally, Robert took this out on the crew, Julio included.

Julio countered by removing all the crucifixes from the engine room and locking himself in his cabin, where he mumbled Rosaries and Hail Marys incessantly. I took this desertion of his beloved engine room to be a bad omen indeed.

"Not to worry," Robert said. He'd take care of the machinery himself. So, armed with a hand grenade and a sledgehammer, he descended into the heat and din of Julio's former domain. The sledgehammer was for delicate adjustments, he said; the grenade for serious malfunctions.

Naturally, the radio and Eduardo's $100,000 satellite navigational system had ceased working soon after we'd left Panama, so the only warning I had of the approaching hurricane was a sudden falling of the barometer and a backing of the wind from northeast to due north.

I checked out our safety equipment: two World War II-vintage inflatable life rafts and a wooden dory slung on davits on the upper deck.

I very casually began to stock the dory with beer and rum.

"What are you doing?"

I turned quickly. It was Jim. "Just stashin' some stuff," I replied, avoiding his eyes.

Jim took a healthy belt of Mount Gay. "You know something the rest of us don't?"

"Weather might kick up a little, is all."

Jim paused, absorbing my statement. "This tub's gonna sink," he said, "and we're all gonna die." He took another slug of rum. "Right?"

"Most likely."

"Robert's gonna get mad when he finds out."

Before I could respond, the ship rocked from a violent explosion somewhere belowdecks.

"Jesus Christ," I said.

"Fucking Robert." Jim shook his head.

We dashed down to the lower deck. Smoke was billowing out of the engine-room door. The ship was listing slightly to port.

Excited Spanish voices issued from the bridge, foredeck, galley and dining salon.

Robert emerged from the engine room coughing and waving away smoke. His eyes were tearing, his face was blackened and he looked about as disheveled as I'd ever seen him. He had the sledgehammer in one hand, a bottle of rum in the other. His hand grenade was conspicuously absent.

"It was an accident," he said.

About twenty minutes later the old *Don Juan* rolled belly-up and sank. All nine of us were crowded into the one raft that could still hold air. The booze-laden dory wallowed a few yards behind, connected to us by a twelve-foot painter.

As the *Don Juan's* bow slid under, Julio let out a joyous whoop. A horrendous weight had been lifted from his shoulders.

A minute or so later the water around us boiled with bubbles. Between two and three thousand marijuana bales popped to the surface, the main cargo hatch having ruptured from air pressure. Hundreds of swimming rats climbed aboard them and commenced to shake dry their fur. This drove High Pockets nuts, but I calmed him down with a handful of Milk Bone Flavor Snacks for Large Dogs.

"Well," Jim said, "at least we didn't lose the load." He passed me the Mount Gay.

It was around sundown when we got picked up. The eastern horizon was black and the wind was rising fast. We had seen the vessel the day before. It was out of Barranquilla on a three-week commercial fishing trip. Luckily they had us on board before they realized that over twenty million dollars' worth of merchandise was floating all around. But darkness closed in and the wind rose quickly to force ten. With tears in his eyes, the skipper turned the ship to the southwest and ran us back to Barranquilla.

Jim had bought several gallons of rum for the ride, so we were all completely blasted when we fell out of the bus and staggered over to Eduardo's favorite Bandito Watering Hole in Riohacha. With the sinking of the *Don Juan*, Julio had lost his religious zeal and was as drunk and rowdy as any of us. He and Robert were getting along famously.

Needless to say, Eduardo wasn't exactly thrilled to see us, but he recovered quickly after Jim spiked his drink with the usual prescription of coke and quaaludes.

"We get a-nother sheep and do eet again!" Eduardo announced.* He then invited us to stay in Riohacha for a week or so of relaxation.

Jim and Robert figured they'd start out where they'd left off before we departed Riohacha three days previously, at least as far as drug consumption was concerned. I was seriously considering abstaining altogether, but I was under intense social pressure so I finally gave in . . .

Everything we call real is made of things that cannot be regarded as real.
—Neils Bohr

---

*Unfortunately, things didn't work out exactly as Eduardo had planned. About two weeks after the *Don Juan* went down, Eduardo got himself into some very hot water with the rest of the Dope Lords in Riohacha. He got drunk one night and was caught in bed with a fellow Dope Lord's wife. This is a serious no-no according to the Dope Lord Code of Conduct. Eduardo blasted his way out of Riohacha and, only slightly wounded, hightailed it for Miami, where he bought a condominium and controlling interest in a local bank.

Eduardo's forced exile raised José from the position of Assistant Dope Lord to Full-Blown Dope Lord, since José is Eduardo's cousin and was his right-hand man. He had held this position nearly three years, until our recent problems (you'll hear all about them by and by) sent the whole lot of us into a financial and legal tailspin. This has resulted in José being demoted to the rank of Full-Blown Bandito, which is several rungs down the ladder from Full-Blown Dope Lord, or even Assistant Dope Lord.

❋ 5 ❋

Big Bang Banditos

Three days ago, around noon on the sixth day after their departure, José and his gang returned from their assault on the University of Barranquilla Research Library. High Pockets and I were involved in a spirited wrestling match in the front yard. Legs was sunning himself on the front steps of the shack. He apparently had a successful night: A lump the size of a billiard ball was moving slowly down his digestive tract.

I had just pulled a quick reversal and had High Pockets pinned to the ground in a slight variation of the doggy-ear hold when I heard hoots and gunshots coming from down the ravine, a sure sign of approaching Banditos.

A few minutes later José emerged from the jungle, his men close behind. Each Bandito carried a leather or sheepskin bag crammed full of books. José carried something large and limp over his right shoulder.

I jumped up and let loose a welcome whoop. High Pockets bounded to José barking and grinning. The Banditos threw down their guns and bags, everybody talking and gesturing. They appeared to have returned more or less intact, although several Banditos sported bandages. José grinned a special Bandito Grin, then dumped what he was carrying (wrapped in a blanket) at my feet. I heard a moan and pulled back the cloth, then looked down in shock at a thin, frail, middle-aged man dressed in a suit. He was bound, gagged, and blindfolded. I surveyed my front lawn—now littered with Banditos, small arms, a few sombreros, hundreds of books and, as it turned out, the head librarian from the University of Barranquilla Research Library.

José and his men stacked the books in front of the shack, forming a wall about twelve feet long, three feet high and two feet thick. José then removed the gag and blindfold from the librarian, whose name turned out to be Señor Rodriguez. The first thing Señor Rodriguez saw as the blindfold was removed was High Pockets' huge pink tongue descending onto his face. Señor Rodriguez was sweating profusely and High Pockets loves the taste of salt. I had to drag him bodily off Señor Rodriguez, who appeared to be experiencing some sort of mild heart attack.

Next, José placed Señor Rodriguez on top of the wall of books and had his gang line up behind it. He then pulled Señor Rodriguez to a sitting position, put his arm around the poor guy's shoulders and instructed me to take a group picture with Tina's father's camera.

I attempted to explain that I still didn't have any film but José insisted that I take a picture anyway.

Over the years I have learned that it's easier to humor José than to reason with him, so I went inside the shack and got the camera.

José and the boys were too close to the shack for me to fit them all in the viewfinder. As soon as I pointed this out I realized I had made a pointless and ridiculous error in judgment.

Fifteen minutes later the Banditos had moved their act ten feet back and posed again. I told them to say *cheso* ("cheese" in Spanish) and snapped the shutter.

I then took José aside and casually inquired about Señor Rodriguez. José explained that Señor Rodriguez was the *jefe* (boss) of the University of Barranquilla Research Library. I waited for him to continue but he just stood there looking very impressed with himself. When I said I didn't understand, José shook his head and frowned at my stupidity.

As it turned out, José and his gang had heisted the books I wanted and then, drunk with power, made off with a couple hundred or so other works (none having anything to do with physics, by the way). Then they'd decided that since I was interested in libraries, I would certainly be interested in the man who ran one.

"Yeah, right. Of course," I thought to myself. This line of reasoning is a perfect example of Bandito Logic, a concept that for some reason is very similar to Female Logic, although, obviously, their roots are quite disparate.

I was then subjected to a rambling account of their exploits. Separating Bandito Fact from Bandito Exaggeration is tough, but the following is a brief, unsensationalized version of José's story.

Here it is: José launched his Bandito Assault early one morning from the east (Banditos like to attack with the sun at their backs). They blasted out the plate-glass windows on one side of the building and piled in (Banditos don't trust doors).

The library had just opened, so Señor Rodriguez was the only person there. This turned out to be a stroke of bad luck for Señor Rodriguez. When José actually *saw* how many books there were, he more or less panicked. He spotted Señor Rodriguez cowering under a desk and dragged him out. At this point a platoon of Colombian troops arrived on the scene and opened up on the library, figuring it had been overrun by terrorists or soccer fans.

José had his men return fire, keeping the troops pinned down, while he forced Señor Rodriguez to collect the books on my list. Once this was accomplished, José and his men bolted to the back of the library, collecting books at random and blasting everything in sight.

The troops countered with mortar fire and grenade launchers. Señor Rodriguez was struck unconscious by a flying volume of the *Works of William Shakespeare* (José caught it on the rebound from Señor Rodriguez's forehead), so José threw him over his shoulder and led his men out of the library via a rear bathroom window. This saved Señor Rodriguez's life, since the troops were unaware that José's Bandito Brigade had escaped and proceeded to blow the University of Barranquilla Research Library to smithereens.

I thanked and congratulated José and the boys, then told José that I'd like a few minutes alone with Señor Rodriguez. I led Señor Rodriguez into the shack and untied him. I had a few belts of mescal, lit a joint, then sat him down and attempted to explain why he was sitting in a shack in the wilds of the Sierra Nevadas, instead of running the University of Barranquilla Research Library.

I started at the beginning, with José's mugging of Tina's family. I explained the situation with respect to Tina's nymphomania (making brief mention of her concealed diaphragm), her betrayal of Tom and Gary, and then got to the crux of the matter: Subatomic Phenomena.

Señor Rodriguez stared at me wide-eyed as I gave him a crash course on the Underlying Nature of Reality. I did this for the same reason I mentioned the Subatomic Realm in my notes to Tom and Gary: I wanted to put Señor Rodriguez's situation in its proper perspective.

I paced the small room, occasionally having a contemplative hit from my joint or a quick belt of mescal. I was about
halfway through a simpleminded discourse on Quantum Mechanics and was preparing to delve into its Many Worlds Interpretation when I realized that Señor Rodriguez had
slumped forward in his chair unconscious. Upon closer inves-
tigation it became evident that he had slipped into some sort
of coma.

This new development was upsetting. I had grown quite
fond of Señor Rodriguez even though, in the few minutes I
knew him as a sentient being, he never spoke a word to me.
What really bothered me was that his comatose condition was
obviously not brought on so much by the bizarre situation he
found himself in as by my explanation of the reasons for it. As
I transferred his limp form from the chair to the bed, I thought
briefly of Tina, Tom, Gary and Tina's father.

I looked out the window. José was romping with High
Pockets while the rest of his crew guzzled tequila and smoked
joints. I yelled for José to come inside.

Presently, he and High Pockets appeared, José with a bottle of tequila in his hand, High Pockets with a volume of the
Book of Knowledge in his mouth.

When I told José what had happened to Señor Rodriguez,
he nodded sagely and said, "Ahh," then bent over and opened
one of Señor Rodriguez's eyes. Nothing but the white was vis-
ible.

Another "Ahh." José then poured about a pint of tequila
down Señor Rodriguez's throat. No reaction. I verified that
there was still a pulse. It seemed strong and steady. José then
slipped off one of Señor Rodriguez's shoes, removed his sock
and proceeded to stick a match between two of his toes. He lit
it and stood back. After a few seconds it had burned down to
the end and gone out. Not a tremor from Señor Rodriguez.

José then agreed that Señor Rodriguez was indeed in some sort of coma.

When I asked him what we were going to do, he told me not to worry. He had a friend who knew an Indian who was familiar with these matters. Naturally it was the same guy who knew the same Indian who was on a crazed fast and wouldn't talk about snakes or Subatomic Particles. When I told José that it was unlikely that the dude would talk about comas either, he scratched himself and sighed. He was stumped, no question about it.

It turned out that neither José nor I felt like attending to a comatose librarian, so we decided to have a few of José's men make a litter and carry Señor Rodriguez back to the University of Barranquilla and dump him in front of the medical center.

José then went outside, gathered his men together and asked for volunteers. None were in the mood to transport Señor Rodriguez back to Barranquilla, a three-day trek through predator infested jungles.

José pulled his .45, pointed it at the Bandito closest to him and asked if he was *sure* he wasn't in the mood. This technique was immediately successful. A few minutes later José and I bid farewell to Señor Rodriguez, then watched him being carried off into the jungle.

I have spent the last three days poring over the books I had requested and received via José's kindness. (I used glue and tape to repair those volumes that had been damaged by shrapnel and small-arms fire.) My mind has been simultaneously boggled and expanded. I am aching for someone to talk to. Someone with whom I can share my insights and wonder. I have decided that only one person in my Universe fits the intellectual bill: Tina's father.

José is still vehemently opposed to a normal correspondence, and I suppose, for security reasons, he's right. So I have settled on a compromise. Tina's father is undoubtedly back in Sausalito by now, so my plan is to send him anonymous musings and ask him to respond via classified ads in the *International Herald Tribune* (a common method of correspondence amongst clandestine operatives). I will ask him to address his ads to "Mr. Quark," Quarks being the most interesting and unpredictable of Subatomic Particles. I'm launching what I hope will be a productive Subatomic Dialogue.

I will now continue the story of how High Pockets and I came to be where we are, starting where I left off, after Robert blew up the Admiral's Inn on Antigua.

> *Those who are not shocked when they first come across quantum theory cannot possibly have understood it.*
>
> —Niels Bohr

✳ **6** ✳

Operation *Looney Tune*

The island I had picked to be our next victim was Curaçao. We weren't too well known there and it was close to Colombia, so José could meet us easily. Since we had lost our last yacht, we had to have a serious sit-down and plan our next move.

We finally got through to him in Riohacha by calling all his favorite Bandito Saloons. The connection was abominable, but we managed to explain our whereabouts and situation.

He showed up the next day at our Holiday Inn. We got very fucked up on drugs and alcohol, then began planning Operation *Looney Tune*.

José had plenty of pot lying around in Colombia, but all our boats had either sunk or been confiscated by various branches of various governments.

Jim suggested that we switch to airplanes, for variety's sake if nothing else. Robert agreed, then suggested that we look up Flash. I was completely against the idea, for reasons that will presently become evident. But the vote was three to one in favor.

We piled into the Lear and headed north, having only vague suspicions as to Flash's whereabouts.

We finally located him on a remote landing strip in the southern Bahamas. Even at 20,000 feet you couldn't miss Flash's World War II–vintage red, white and blue B-29 bomber.

Harry put the Lear down on the hard coral strip and taxied up to Flash's plane, appropriately named the *Looney Tune*.

He and his dog, Aileron, were passed out in the shade under the portside wing. High Pockets and Aileron had a joyous doggy reunion, but I was wary. Flash always makes me nervous, to tell you the truth.

Flash is the most unbalanced of all my associates. He had found the B-29 in a heap at the end of a jungle landing strip in Colombia after crashing his old DC-3. He has no pilot's license and never will, I'm sure. His flaming red hair is tied in a ponytail and matches his handlebar mustache. The B-29, which he had put back together with coat hangers and baling wire, was his airborne version of a hippie VW bus. He even fitted it with a crude kitchen and waterbed. The *Looney Tune* was his home.

He is an itinerant Contrabandista who works on one-shot contracts, usually to down-and-out desperadoes like our group. You had to be desperate to even go near that dude. I'll give you an example of Flash's twisted Worldview. As a pilot, Flash has his own Theory of Gravitation. He feels that if he gets stoned enough during a flight, gravity will have less effect on him, and therefore on the airplane, thereby increasing lift, decreasing drag and saving fuel. A result of his theory is that Flash is unconcerned about running out of gas. It always comes as a surprise to him when the engines die at 10,000 feet. He's dispensed with fuel gauges altogether, as a matter of fact, claiming they are a distraction. In place of navigational instruments, Flash has a Betamax mounted in the cockpit.

Flash has a sense of humor, though. Whenever the *Looney*

Tune coughs and dies in midair, he'll yell back to Aileron in a perfect Porky Pig imitation, "The-ah, the-ah, that's all folks!"

The *Looney Tune* was in appalling condition, as one might suspect. It had one hell of a sound system, though. Flash likes to listen to the Doors or Jefferson Airplane while he and Aileron roar over hill and dale (at treetop level to avoid radar), the cockpit dense with marijuana smoke. Or if he's familiar with the terrain, he'll watch vintage cartoons on the Betamax.

Anyway, we revived Flash, cracked open a case of bubbly and got down to some serious conspiring. I dimly recall the basic plan. High Pockets and I had a couple hundred hours in various vintage airplanes (mostly DC-3's and -4's) and would be, respectively, copilot and navigator (navigation not being one of Flash's fortes). Aileron is Flash's tailgunner, so he'd sit in the tailgunner's bubble and keep lookout for bogies.

With the help of the Mayor of Santa Marta, José would re-open Santa Marta International Airport at precisely midnight the following Sunday and have 5,000 pounds of gold buds waiting on the runway. After the pickup—with José, Jim and Robert flying escort in the Lear—Flash and I would fly north to Bimini, where we'd refuel, then continue on to Massachusetts, where some of Flash's burnt-out buddies still ran a commune. We'd airdrop the bales onto them and land at a nearby county airport, where José, Jim and Robert would be waiting.

It sounded pretty much foolproof, but unfortunately things didn't work out exactly as we planned.

Quantum weirdness is not only real—it is observable.
—John Gribbin

Schrödinger's Bandito

A week or so ago we had some excitement up here. It came in the form of a platoon of Colombian troops. José claims they were looking for me, but I suspect their visit had something to do with his pillaging of the University of Barranquilla Research Library. Maybe it was a combination of the two. Possibly Señor Rodriguez came out of his coma, identified High Pockets and me through mug shots, then remembered enough about the area to more or less pinpoint our location. At any rate, José and his crew treated them to a typical Bandito Welcome—in other words, with guns blazing.

The battle was apparently short but spirited. (I only *heard* it, so this information is secondhand.) José claims he had a great time playing with his rocket launcher (the one he had used on the jaguar) and doubts that we'll have any further problems with the army or anyone else in his right mind.

A couple days after the shoot-out, there was another interesting development, right here at my shack. José's buddy who knows the Indian on the crazed fast informed José that the Indian is eating and talking again. José asked me if I'd like to meet the guy to discuss snakes, Subatomic Phenomena, comas or anything else. I said sure, why not?

So José showed up with this wizened Guajiran clad in a loincloth and festooned with feathers, bones, amulets and two Timex watches. José explained that the old geezer was a holy man of some sort, and that he'd been fasting in order to reach a higher plane or whatever.

Luckily the old Indian spoke Spanish, so I asked José if I could spend some time alone with him. José nodded sagely, mounted his little burro and disappeared into the jungle.

I gave the guy a banana, which he swallowed whole, peel and all, and then motioned for him to sit down. He squatted on the floor.

I wanted to find out exactly how wise he was before delving into important issues, so first I asked him why it was that High Pockets and Legs seemed to get along fairly well except on Wednesdays.

He nodded and explained he would have to meet them. Since it was Saturday I figured there wouldn't be any problem with this.

I called for High Pockets to come out from under the bed. He emerged bleary-eyed, yawned, then erupted in a short sneezing attack. I told him to sit down in front of the old Indian.

In order to roust Legs from his nest under the shack, I picked up my M-16, rammed home a clip and fired a few bursts out the window. I then placed the rifle in front of the old Indian and High Pockets. Legs appeared on cue, snaked his way up the warm barrel and dozed off.

The old Indian placed one hand on High Pockets' head, lightly gripped Legs with the other and closed his eyes.

He sat that way for about ten minutes. Neither he nor Legs nor High Pockets moved a muscle. I had never seen High Pockets sit so still. He didn't even blink. Legs didn't blink either, but I attributed this to the fact that snakes don't have eyelids.

Finally the old Indian opened his eyes and put his hands on his bony knees.

He then explained that the phenomenon was astrological in nature. It had to do with, among other things, phases of the moon in conjunction with the birth signs of Legs and High Pockets. (Guajiran astrology involves well over 500 birth signs.)

I smirked inwardly and reminded him that the lunar cycle is twenty-eight days and our monthly calendar (excluding February) has thirty or thirty-one. This would result in Wednesday falling on different phases of the moon each month, so what the fuck did the moon have to do with anything, for chrissakes?

The old Indian smiled slightly, motioned for me to calm down and proceeded to impress the hell out of me with a detailed discourse on how the retrograde motions of certain planets (most notably Mars) coupled with the Coriolis effect* caused High Pockets' doggy consciousness to conflict arhythmically with Legs's consciousness, which is, he added, longer and narrower than High Pockets' consciousness, even though a dog's spirit is located in his tail. He then explained that dogs don't really wag their tails but that the Great Spirit is moving in such a way that when dogs wag their tails, the tails are really stationary while everything else wags.

At this point I sensed he was starting to ramble in order to distract me from some glaring inconsistencies in his answer to the original question.

---

*The Indian didn't call it by name, but he was clearly referring to this phenomenon, which has to do with the rotation of the earth and its effects on fluid or gaseous bodies.

For example: Legs was not born—he was hatched. And as impressed as I was with the old Indian's knowledge of astronomy, and most especially of the Coriolis effect, much of his astrological data still rang untrue.

Now I was in a quandary. I wanted to get down to more serious matters, namely, Subatomic Phenomena, but I wasn't sure that the old Indian was ready or willing to absorb the profundity of what I had to say, never mind add some insights of his own.

I had a couple belts of mescal to clear my head.

What the hell? I figured. I'll give it a shot.

I casually inquired if he would care to hear my views on the Underlying Nature of Reality. His nod was barely perceptible.

I started at the beginning, with José's mugging of Tina's family. I explained how my newfound wisdom was somehow related to Tina's nymphomania (I didn't mention the concealed diaphragm since it is doubtful that Indians are familiar with such devices), then briefly described José's assault on the University of Barranquilla Research Library and the abduction of Señor Rodriguez. I asked him his views on comas. He closed his eyes for a few seconds, then told me he thought comas were okay. I was impressed by the almost poetic brevity of this answer, so I decided to dive headlong into the New Physics.

I felt that the old Indian needed a bit of background information, so I first gave a very brief but insightful lecture on the history of science, physics in particular. I made mention of Copernicus, Galileo and, most importantly, Newton.

I explained how Newton's laws of motion and gravitation had formed the bedrock of classical physics. Laws that we take for granted. Laws that we either learned in high school or know intuitively. Laws that deal with cause and effect. Laws that say that the Universe is an orderly and predictable place. Laws that have been found to be totally untrue.

I paused for effect. There didn't appear to be any. The old

Indian was still sitting on the floor impassively. I smiled to myself. See what I mean? I thought. A cause with no effect.

I lit a joint. Exhaled contemplatively.

"Then came Einstein," I said. I knew I was getting a little out of whack chronologically, but the old Indian was a tough audience, so I figured I'd better get to the crux of the matter. I explained how Einstein's Theories of Relativity (General and Special) had thrown classical physics on its ear, setting the stage for the next revolution in modern thought and science: Quantum Mechanics.*

At this point the old Indian asked for another banana. Again, he shoved it down his throat without peeling or chewing it. I got the distinct feeling that he was trying to derail my train of thought.

"No more bananas until I'm through," I warned. His nod was barely perceptible.

I had another warning to lay on the old Indian. This was it: We were about to make a conceptual leap. A leap from the Macrocosmic world of Bananas and Banditos to the bizarre Realm of the Atom and Beyond. We were about to take a look at what's really going on. A leap from here to *here*, as it were.

I was starting to get excited, so I had a few more belts of mescal to calm myself down. I relit my joint.

I then explained that one of the major problems with discussing the world beneath the atom is that our language is geared for Macrocosmic Reality and that the best way to understand the Microcosmic Realm is to use allusions, metaphors and analogies. Otherwise, what we call "common sense" can short-circuit our acceptance of the Truth.**

---

*The ultimate irony is that Einstein, one of the founding fathers of Quantum Theory (although he didn't know it at the time), could never bring himself to accept it.
**I call this language problem the "Concept of the Dangling Subatomic Participle." It is a problem we can never escape from.

The first thing I did was to guide the old Indian down the path from Macrocosmic Reality to the nitty-gritty world of Underlying Reality. I started by explaining that a long, long time ago there was Nothing. No space, no time, no matter. Zip. Doodley Squat. Then there was a Bang. A very Big Bang.* The Universe actualized and expanded rapidly, forming a Space-Time Continuum. Matter and energy appeared, stars and solar systems formed, along with the aforementioned Banditos and Bananas. Upon hearing the word "bananas" the old Indian cleared his throat.

Okay, I thought to myself. He wants to fuck around with me. Well, two can play that game.

I grabbed a banana and held it up. "What are bananas made of?" The old Indian licked his lips.

"Banana stuff," he replied. This was more or less what I'd hoped he would say. Now I figured I really had him.

"And what is banana stuff made of," I inquired smugly.

The old Indian's response to this question took me by surprise. "The Great Spirit," he answered without hesitation.

I took a big hit from my joint. Exhaled contemplatively.

"And what is the Great Spirit made of?"

He put his hand on High Pockets' head. High Pockets wagged his tail, as he always does in response to a display of affection. "Ask his tail," the old Indian replied.

"What?" I was getting annoyed again.

The old Indian smiled, his eyes fixed on the banana I was holding. "The Great Spirit wags," he said. "Now give me the banana."**

---

*The astute reader is obviously aware that since there was nothing before the Big Bang, the adjective "big" is suspect. I admit there were no Small Bangs to compare it with, but as I said I'm struggling with language here.
**In some sense the old Indian was right. Metaphorically, the Great Spirit *does* wag, but I was too pissed off to realize this.

"No bananas, goddammit!" I yelled. "Abso-fucking-lutely no bananas!"

I had a monumental belt of mescal, then handed the bottle to the old Indian. "You get the banana when I say you get the banana."

His nod was barely perceptible. He drained the half-full bottle in one slug.

"Jesus Christ," I said.

The old Indian let fly an incredible belch, scaring the shit out of High Pockets, who bounded out the door and into the jungle. Even Legs was startled.

"All right, all right," I said, trying to calm things down.

At this point, the old Indian started giggling. Apparently the mescal was kicking in.

I sighed and sat down. "Are you in touch with the Great Spirit?" I asked.

The old Indian nodded and continued to giggle.

"Tell him to go fuck himself," I said.

My comment had the desired effect. The old Indian stopped giggling and closed his eyes.

"I am now going to tell you all about this Great Spirit of yours," I boasted. "Banana Stuff or any other kind of stuff is made of atoms, in the case of bananas, mostly carbon atoms. Now, when we get further down, below the level of the atom, things get weird."

I started pacing in front of the old Indian, who remained immobile, his eyes still shut.

"There is only one system of thought that has successfully explained the nature of Subatomic Phenomena," I continued. "That system of thought is called Quantum Mechanics. It is a way of looking at Underlying Reality. It is a way of looking at your Great Spirit."

At this, the old Indian's eyeballs started rolling around behind his eyelids, as if he were in REM sleep. As if he were having a spectacular dream or hallucination.

"Your Great Spirit is a very bad boy. He has been doing his best to confuse us. But we have more or less figured out what he is up to. He has given us an apparently orderly Universe. But under that illusory order, there is chaos. Absurdity."

I relit my joint and continued. I went on to explain how Quantum Theory has demolished our conception of causality, of the connectedness of events.

"Moreover, Subatomic Units, the stuff everything is made of, do not behave like solid particles. Instead, they behave like abstract entities. Statistical entities that have *tendencies* to exist."

I held the banana in front of the old Indian's closed eyes.

"In some sense, this is an illusion. We conjure up reality and reality conjures us up. You participate in the existence of this banana and vice versa. This Great Spirit you are talking about is mathematically described by Quantum Mechanics. This mathematics indicates that chance is absolute. The Great Spirit doesn't know what the fuck he's doing."

The old Indian opened his eyes slowly and stared straight ahead.

"Matter, indeed, the whole of the Universe, is essentially nonsubstantial. In other words, there is no Banana Stuff in the real sense. Simplistically speaking, this banana is 'made' of waves and these waves are probability waves. To put it another way, this banana *probably* exists. Do you still want it?"

The old Indian didn't move a muscle.

"I thought not." I opened another bottle of mescal and had a belt. "The human view that we live in a Universe that 'makes sense' is gone forever. The whole thing is a Cosmic Crapshoot. The first rule is that there *are* no rules and the rules and the paradoxes go on and on and the circus goes on and on with an infinite number of acts, sideshows and freaks."

I heard a faint humming sound. It was coming from the old Indian.

High Pockets started howling from the jungle.

Legs was staring at the old Indian from his position wrapped around my M-16.

"Now we come to the problem of Schrödinger's Bandito."*

The humming increased in intensity by a few decibels.

"Let's assume that José was captured during his assault on the University of Barranquilla Research Library and was thrown into solitary confinement by the Army.

"Let us further assume that a sadistic Generalissimo has placed a vial of deadly nerve gas in José's cell. A random event (like whether or not a uranium atom decays during a specific time period) will decide whether the gas is released."

At this point I digressed slightly. I explained that the work of Heisenberg, Schrödinger and others had led to the afore-mentioned conclusion that we are *participators* in the reality we are stuck with, not observers. Extrapolating from this, it has come to be accepted that nothing really occurs until it is observed; in this case by the Generalissimo. When he looks in the jail cell he will observe that José is either alive or dead. He will then know that the uranium atom has decayed. Again, until this observation, *nothing has happened.*

The old Indian's humming was getting louder.

"Let's say the Generalissimo is fucking his girlfriend and doesn't get around to checking how José is doing for an hour after the allotted time. What is José's status during this hour? Common sense tells us that he is either alive or dead."

I paused for emphasis. "Quantum Theory says that this is simply not the case. The Copenhagen Interpretation asserts

---

*The problem is really called "Schrödinger's Cat," but I figured the old Indian could relate better to Banditos.

that José is neither alive nor dead, but is in some sort of limbo, waiting to be observed."

It now became necessary to raise my voice. Between High Pockets' howling outside and the old Indian's humming inside, I could hardly hear myself think.

"This idea that José's condition is contingent upon a horny Generalissimo's sexual endurance runs against the grain of many scientists. John Wheeler, Hugh Everett and Neill Graham came up with a nifty solution to the dilemma."

Now I was yelling. "The orthodox interpretation of Quantum Mechanics says that one of the possibilities actualizes. José is either alive or dead. What Wheeler, Everett and Graham propose is that *both* actualize, but in *two different branches of reality!*"

The old Indian's humming was now wavering like a police car siren. High Pockets' howling was more or less in tune with him.

Legs got disgusted with the situation and snaked his way back down to the floor, then disappeared through his crack.

"The Edition of José that is eventually observed (for sentimental reasons, let's say he's alive) is the Edition of José in our Reality. In some other Branch of Reality, there is an Edition of José that is dead! This theory is appropriately called the Many Worlds Interpretation of Quantum Mechanics!"*

I took another serious slug of mescal, then screamed over the din, "How's your Great Spirit doing, Jack?"

The old Indian abruptly stopped humming. High Pockets shut his trap, too. The resulting total silence made me a little woozy. Maybe it was the mescal. It's hard to say.

---

*If this sounds like nonsense, let me remind the reader of some other examples of theories that were nonsense:

The earth is round (Eratosthenes, 300 B.C.)
Man will someday fly (L. da Vinci, 15th century)

I examined the old Indian's eyes. It was obvious that he was in some sort of trance. I thought briefly of Señor Rodriguez, wherever he was, then of Tina, Tom, Gary and Tina's father.

The old Indian suddenly rose and walked stiffly out of the shack and disappeared into the jungle. I haven't seen him since.*

This morning I woke up with a monumental idea buzzing around in my head. Since Tina's father has not responded to my missive, I've decided that some drastic action has to be taken. Something that will shake him up enough to force a response. I have also decided to include Tina, Tom and Gary in my plan. I will drop notes at regular intervals to the whole group.

This new volley of musings will be Subatomic in nature, and I have hatched an ingenious plan to keep them all on their conceptual toes. José has agreed to help me in this. He has Bandito Cohorts all over South and Central America, a veritable Bandito Grapevine. He will have his Bandito Buddies mail my notes from many different Bandito Strongholds *simultaneously*. The handwriting and my unmistakable style and wit will be the

---

The earth is not the center of the universe (N. Copernicus, 16th century)
Motion is relative (A. Einstein, early 20th century)
Girls just wanna have fun (C. Lauper, late 20th century)

The list goes on and on. The point is that "nonsense" is only that which *appears* to be unintelligible from *our* present point of view. Let me also add that the principles of Quantum Physics have passed every experimental test yet devised and have led to the development of, among other things, transistor radios, pocket calculators, microcomputers, and some revolutionary new heat-seeking, cordless sexual aids.

*This is a Time Travel Footnote (TTF). I am contacting you from the future. Exactly how far in the future is none of your business, although you will find out eventually. I zipped back here to tell you what I have just learned about the old Indian. He is back on his crazed fast and hasn't eaten, talked or moved for several months.

same, so it will appear that I am in many different places at the *same instant!*

The astute reader should immediately sense the similarity between this concept and the Many Worlds Interpretation of Quantum Mechanics (each note will metaphorically represent a different Edition of me). I am especially interested in Tina's father's reaction. I can't wait to see if he picks up on what I am doing. I am, in essence, putting his Subatomic Mettle to the acid test.

God only knows what Tina, Tom and Gary will think of all this.

> *If one has to stick to this damned quantum jumping, then I regret having ever become involved in this thing.*
>
> —Erwin Schrödinger

✳ 8 ✳

The Flight of the *Looney Tune*

Flash and I took off from the Bahamas and headed for Colombia, accompanied by our two Canine Cohorts in Crime. At my insistence we had filled his waterbed with high octane AV-gas and hooked up a transfer pump to the *Looney Tune*'s fuel tanks. Flash made me edgy by throwing lit roaches over his shoulder, in the general direction of his volatile bed.

In spite of the fact that the *Looney Tune* had no navigational equipment other than a crude compass, we managed to find Santa Marta International. Flash did one of his patented roller-coaster landings, causing José's gang of Bandito onloaders to erupt in spontaneous applause.

José, Robert, Jim, Flash and I relaxed on the runway while the Banditos loaded up the plane. We got into some serious drinking while High Pockets and Aileron (doggy buddies of the first order) wandered off, doing whatever dogs do when they are out of sight of human beings.

When José's crew finished the onload, they joined us for a bon voyage party.

Flash and I collected the dogs and staggered into the *Looney Tune*. Flash turned the stereo up to full blast, lit a joint, then did one of his crowd-pleaser takeoffs. We headed north, climbing very slowly since we were dangerously overloaded.

About an hour out of Santa Marta, we leveled off at 10,000 feet. High Pockets, Flash and I were crowded together in the cluttered cockpit since the rest of the plane was jammed full of fifty-pound marijuana bales. As mentioned previously, Aileron's post was all the way aft in the tailgunner's bubble.

"Aileron!" Flash called out between hits on his spliff. A single muffled bark was the response.

"All clear?"

Two barks. This was the all-clear signal. Three barks meant that Aileron had spotted another plane. One that was on a heading different from ours. Sort of a yellow alert. Four or more barks meant that the bogie had changed course in our direction or that he had spotted one that was definitely shadowing us. This was red alert. Hysterical howling meant we were in deep shit—say, being fired on by a fighter plane—and would have to take drastic action.

This usually took the form of a steep dive toward whatever land was nearby so Flash could weave his way between hills, trees or (his favorite) buildings in order to shake his foe.

"Old Aileron's got a sixth sense about bogies," Flash explained as he raised the volume on his massive sound system, then adjusted the color-tuning on the Beta.

The cockpit was awash in marijuana smoke eerily illuminated by a Road Runner cartoon. Jim Morrison was bellowing "Backdoor Man."

"One time old Aileron heard this F-16 coming before he actually saw it." He passed me the joint.

"I put the *Tune* into a radical dive to treetop level, found some city—ah, Baltimore, I think—it's hard to tell. Which is the one with all the statues and monuments?"

"That's Washington."

A contemplative pause. "No shit. I shoulda been over Baltimore," Flash grunted. "Tailwinds."

I pointed out that we were somewhat off course. In fact, we were headed in the general direction of Portugal.

"Oh, yeah. Right."

"You see that star, the sorta faint one at the end of the Little Dipper?" I asked, waving smoke from the windscreen.

"Little Dipper?"

"That's Polaris, the North Star. Put our nose on that and leave it there. Our course is almost directly true north."

"Far out." The fact that Flash had never heard of Polaris made me edgier than I already was.

Flash seemed to sense my growing apprehensions. "Don't worry. Soon's we get down to treetop level, we'll be OK."

Let me add at this point that Flash is the only living aviator who feels safer at low altitude. At high altitudes not only is navigation easier (due to increased visibility) but in the event of engine failure, it's possible to glide to a reasonably safe emergency landing. Moreover, flying at treetop level is, almost by definition, a questionable practice. A small lapse in concentration at 200 or so miles per hour can quickly turn a treetop below you into a full-blown tree in front of you.

Flash's response to this inescapable logic was this: "Bullshit. The higher you come, the farther you fall. It's an old aviator's saying."

"Wait a minute," I said. "The old saying is, 'The *bigger* they come, the *harder* they fall.' It doesn't have anything to do with aviation."

A contemplative pause. "Treetop level," Flash mumbled,

then turned the stereo up full blast, making further conversation impossible.

We reached the Bahamas at first light, located Bimini and landed. Our Learjet was in front of the ramshackle customs shed. Robert and Jim were drunk and arguing with the police chief and two customs officers. They wanted $10,000 more than the usual fee for refueling a pot-laden airplane. José had brought his Thompson submachine gun and wanted to settle the dispute in the prescribed Bandito Fashion, but I talked him out of it.

The situation finally calmed down sufficiently for us to get the *Looney Tune* fueled up. We took off, leaving Robert, José and Jim waving magnums of bubbly on the runway.

Harry and the copilot had stayed in the Lear the whole time, as usual. In spite of his impressive war record, Harry claimed that some of our antics made him nervous, so he preferred not to get involved.

We had timed the flight so we could make the Massachusetts coast as night fell.

I got a little tense when I realized that we were over Nova Scotia and (I calculated) getting low on fuel.

Flash didn't seem concerned. "Crosswinds," he mumbled, then hung a sharp left and proceeded to follow the jagged coastline at treetop level.

I turned down the stereo. "I think we could use a tad more altitude."

Flash gave her more throttle, clipped the top of a pine tree, relit his joint and grinned. "Treetop level."

I looked at High Pockets. He was lying on a bale, his eyes shut tight.

"Aileron!" Flash called out.

One bark.

"All clear?"

Two barks.

I was the bombardier. Flash gave me the "bombs away" thumbs-up signal when he figured we were over his buddies' commune. I snapped open the bomb bay doors, then, to my horror, realized that High Pockets was still lying on top of the bale with his eyes shut.

What I next perceived was obviously a hallucination, probably brought on by a combination of breathing marijuana smoke and watching Road Runner cartoons for more than ten hours with two dogs and one outright lunatic.

Anyway, the bale High Pockets was lying on dropped into the night with a hundred or so others, but High Pockets remained suspended over the open bomb bay, his eyes still closed.

After what seemed like an eternity, he opened his eyes, looked down, realized there was nothing under him but air, then managed to scramble, Wile E. Coyote style, from the brink of doom.

My relief at High Pockets' escape from certain death was short-lived.

"Why is it so quiet?" I asked myself out loud.

Flash looked over his shoulder, grinned, then subjected me to his Porky Pig impression. The last thing I remember about the flight of the *Looney Tune* was the weird expression on High Pockets' face and my own realization that it was so quiet because the engines had quit. I was then struck by flying debris and lost consciousness.

We weren't over the commune, as it turned out. But we *were* out of gas and several government agencies had amassed all over the state, waiting for us.

Flash and I were taken into custody after gravity did its thing with respect to the *Looney Tune*.

Apparently we had been under intense scrutiny for quite a

while. Some of the agencies (the Drug Enforcement Administration, for example) had no idea that other agencies (the CIA,
for example) were also on our case, so things got very confused
and twisted.

Meanwhile, José, Robert and Jim had heard us roar over
the commune and had jumped into our Rider rental truck to
find the new drop zone.

Evidently the movie had just started when Flash gave me
the drop sign, causing our load to be strewn across a crowded
drive-in theater. The audience was quite enthusiastic about this
gift from above.

José copped a heavy Bandito Attitude when he saw the de-
lighted moviegoers loading our bales into the trunks of their
cars and roaring off. He jumped out of the truck, his Thompson machine gun blazing warning shots. The boys managed to
salvage about half the load and escaped before the local authorities figured out what was going on.

Everybody was curious about Flash's and my whereabouts,
so they drove back to the commune and turned on the news.
This was a common method we used to find out what happened when things didn't go exactly as planned.

The boys got upset when the newscaster informed them
that Flash, High Pockets, Aileron and I were in the clink.

*You live in a deranged age, more deranged than usual, because in spite of
great scientific and technological advances, man has not the faintest idea
of who he is or what he is doing.* —Walker Percy

✳ **9** ✳

Bandito Baseball

Our little shack in the jungle has turned into a veritable Temple of Cosmic Enlightenment. As my understanding of the wonderful machinations of this Universe of ours increases, so does my serenity. I am dragging High Pockets down the Path of Canine Quiescence with the Leash of Knowledge.

I would like to make this world a mellower, more peaceful place for all God's children. Last week I decided to begin my Crusade for World Peace right here in my own little Corner of the Cosmos. José and his boys have started a feud with a gang of Rival Banditos from the other side of the mountain. Some sort of primitive territorial imperative is at the bottom of it, I suspect.

Anyway, I decided to begin my crusade by giving José and his gang some insight into the Underlying Nature of Reality, thereby putting the dispute in its proper perspective. I persuaded José to let High Pockets and me visit the village for a night of pool and mescal. I prepared a lecture, loaded my M-16 and rode down into town on Pepe's cousin, a little burro named Raoul.

The town is more or less your typical Bandito Stronghold: a narrow, unpaved road with a few adobe houses and shops on either side, some corrals containing various forms of livestock (mostly pigs, goats and chickens), along with several mortar emplacements and a .30-caliber machine gun nest in the steeple of the town's rarely visited church. The night I showed up, the town's old diesel generator was on the blink, so the street was dimly lit by a few kerosene torches and a bonfire in front of Enrique's Astoria del Waldorfo, the town's Bandito Saloon. I dismounted Raoul and entered Enrique's place, ready to get down to some serious Subatomic Business. Unfortunately, the evening didn't go exactly as I had planned.

The saloon was well lit by flickering kerosene lamps and packed with Banditos, who were also well lit. I hadn't seen most of the gang since their return from assaulting the University of Barranquilla Research Library, so High Pockets and I got a rousing Bandito Welcome—in other words, with guns blazing (through the roof).

I was forced to chug a pint of homemade mescal (a house rule) before I could order a drink from the bar.

A chaotic pool game was in progress. José was roaring drunk and brandishing a broken pool cue. He was chasing one of his men around the table, bellowing Bandito Threats while his drunken cohorts yelled encouragement and made bets. Rowdy Banditos make High Pockets nervous, so he slinked over to an unoccupied corner and lay down.

José flung what was left of the cue stick in the general direction of the bar, pulled his .45, shot a hole through the pool table, then, apparently having forgotten why he was pissed off at the other Bandito, embraced him, laughing hysterically.

They both toppled over onto a table, pissing off some Banditos who were playing dominoes. This resulted in a Bandito Chain Reaction that got everyone in the place pissed off. High Pockets and I saw it coming and bolted outside. A Bandito Brawl is an awesome sight if one isn't used to random destruction.*

Anyway, as in all chain reactions, the Bandito Brawl wound down slowly. The crashing and grunting sounds from within the Astoria del Waldorfo abated as well as the frequency and velocity of Flying Banditos.

Eventually José emerged from inside. He stood on the stoop holding a liter of mescal in one hand and his tattered sombrero in the other. He looked about as drunk and disheveled as I'd ever seen him. He took a huge belt of mescal, tossed his damaged sombrero into the street, then yelled for High Pockets and me to come inside for a drink.

We zigzagged our way back to the saloon, trying to avoid stepping on unconscious and semiconscious Banditos, and entered. José followed us in, calling out for Enrique to come out from wherever he was hiding. He emerged cautiously from under the bar. Needless to say, his place was a shambles.

José offered me the only intact bar stool and ordered a round on the house for the two of us, plus a plate of rice, beans and salsa for High Pockets.

I then explained that I had some vital topics to discuss with him and his men.

---

*Bandito Behavior, Bandito Brawls in particular, are very similar to certain aspects of the Subatomic Realm. For example, in most experimental situations, one never sees the actual mechanism of the events that lead to an experimental result (we may see evidence an electron did such and such, but never "see" the actual electron or what it did en route to the result). From our position as observers outside the bar, High Pockets and I could not see the random chaos inside (let's say the Banditos represent excited electrons) but we could see the results of the chaos: Every few seconds a Bandito would fly through a window or out the door (each Flying Bandito representing an electron striking a photographic plate or other measuring device).

He slugged down the remainder of his mescal and inquired as to what these topics might be.

When I replied that they involved the Underlying Nature of Reality and how it related to his gang's feud with the Rival Full-Blown Bandito on the other side of the mountain, he said, "Ahh," nodded sagely, then excused himself. He stumbled out onto the porch and discharged a round from his .45, meanwhile yelling at the top of his lungs for any Bandito within earshot to get his ass back into Enrique's Astoria del Waldorfo.

In a few minutes the saloon was packed with woozy Banditos, some bleeding from cuts and contusions sustained during the brawl.

In order to make Quantum Theory comprehensible to a score or so of cranky Banditos, I knew I had to lay some groundwork.

I had José and his crew gather around the pool table.* I then racked the balls and commenced my lecture on classical Newtonian physics. The old physics that had led scientists to the erroneous conclusion that the universe is a predictable and orderly place. I was, of course, going to use the pool table and its caroming balls as a metaphor for Newton's cause-and-effect Worldview.

I explained that according to Newton all natural phenomena are innately predictable if we have enough information about mass, momentum, direction of movement, etc. To demonstrate, I set the cue ball in front of the rack and, before taking aim, explained about angles of incidence and reflection and how, according to the old physics, if we knew enough about my break shot, we could predict where each

---

*By the way, I have made an informal study of Bandito Pool Tables. They all have one thing in common: No matter where you hit a ball, it dribbles into the corner pocket nearest the bar.

ball would end up when friction and air resistance caused it to stop.

My demonstration didn't work out exactly as I had planned. I put a little too much English on my break shot, causing it to fly off the pack and across the room.

The cue ball described a parabolic trajectory that was terminated by José's forehead. Following the laws pertaining to momentum and reflection, the errant shot ricocheted off José's head, then a wall, broke a bottle of mescal that a Bandito was raising to his lips, then shattered a kerosene lamp, causing a minor conflagration behind the bar.

High Pockets panicked and bolted outside.

Enrique panicked and threw a pot of black bean soup on the fire.

José's gang erupted in uproarious laughter.

José himself toppled over backward onto the floor. He was out cold.

I was momentarily at a loss for words. I checked José. I had really rung his bell: A lump the size of a golf ball had already blossomed on his forehead and was obviously intent on further expansion.

I knew I had to act quickly to regain my credibility.

"You see!" I yelled over the laughter. "I was just getting to the point! Newton could never have predicted this! A random event!"*

I grabbed a grease pencil from my pocket and scrawled in huge letters on the wall: "RE."

"RE! A random event!" I then wrote the equals sign (=). "Equals a UB, an Unconscious Bandito!" I underlined the equation. "RE = UB."

I had a slug of mescal and rambled on. "This equation

---

*The astute reader is obviously aware that I was completely winging it at this point.

forms the very foundation of Quantum Theory!'"* I headed for the door. "I will continue the lecture another time!" With that, I collected High Pockets and hauled ass back to the shack. I had no idea what kind of mood José would be in when he regained consciousness, and even less desire to find out.

On the way back, I decided to rethink my plan to stop further violence between José's gang and their rivals on the other side of the mountain.

José showed up at the shack the next day. Sure enough, the lump on his forehead had moved on from golf to tennis.

Luckily for me, my errant break shot had resulted in José sustaining a mild concussion and a slight case of Bandito Amnesia. He recalled nothing of my aborted lecture on Newtonian physics or being knocked senseless by the flying cue ball. His crew, God bless them, had had enough compassion for me and regard for my friendship with José not to blow the whistle.

Anyway, during the night I had devised a plan to peacefully settle the Bandito Dispute.

After much haggling and negotiating, José and his Rival Full-Blown Bandito agreed to go along with my plan.

I proposed that the two gangs compete in a sporting event, the winners of which would be dubbed the Best Banditos. I picked baseball since it isn't too heavy a contact sport and probably wouldn't cause too many Bandito Temper Flare-Ups, which can be lethal. Unfortunately, the game didn't go exactly as I had planned.

---

*(Another TTF: Time Travel Footnote) Again, I am contacting you from the future and, again, it is none of your business from how far in the future I am speaking. My message is this: Recent experiences (you'll hear all about them by and by) have led me to the conclusion that my improvised equation, $RE = UB$, may actually be, metaphorically at least, right on the money.

Miraculously, nobody was killed, but several Banditos from both teams were wounded and I suffered a mild concussion* when, as umpire of the event, I made a bad call at the plate in the top of the first inning. I ejected the Bandito who hit me with the bat from the game, even though he was on José's team.

The actual gun battle didn't start until the bottom of the fifth. I called the game a tie (José's team was 22 runs ahead) and beat a hasty retreat.

The real news, the big news, doesn't have anything to do with Bandito Baseball, however. It happened yesterday and my heartbeat still has not returned to its normal rhythm.

Are you ready? All right. Here it is: I heard from Tina's father.

I suggest the reader take a breather at this point in order to allow the implications of this to sink in.

It is now obvious to me, though I had suspected it all along, that my life is linked to Tina's father's in some weird Subatomic sort of way. But in my completely serene state of mind, I do not try to question. I make decisions in the mundane world of Bandito Baseball Games, but when it comes down to the Big Riddle, when the Cosmic Bandito slides into a close play at the Home Plate of Enlightenment, who am I to judge or analyze?

In my original note to Tina's father I had instructed him to contact me as "Mr. Quark" in an *International Trib* ad, Quarks being the most elusive (illusory?) of Subatomic Particles. Subsequently, as you will recall, I had José's Bandito Buddies mail cryptic messages to him (plus Tom, Gary and Tina) from various Bandito Strongholds in order to see if he would understand my reference to the Many Worlds Interpretation of Quantum

---

*If the reader considers it a coincidence that both José and I suffered mild concussions within a few days of each other, while I was trying to peacefully settle Bandito Disputes, he or she has obviously missed something along the way.

Mechanics. Tina's father's response was more enlightened than I could ever have expected. This is what he said in the ad: "Mr. Quark: Please leave me and my family alone."

Quarks are extraordinarily elusive particles (as many now known particles were in the past) with some strange characteristics.

—Gary Zukav

✳ 10 ✳

Every Silver Lining
Has A Cloud*

Various federal agencies squab-
bled amongst themselves, each wanting to be the first to inter-
rogate Flash and myself. High Pockets and Aileron were given
a private cell. I assumed that a Canine Constable of some sort
would eventually get around to them.

Flash was almost strangled with his own ponytail by a
crazed Federal Aviation Administration official who had apparently been chasing him for years. Flash's infamous B-29 was evidently a legend amongst air traffic controllers; it had caused
several nervous breakdowns and was said to have been a bar-
gaining point when they recently attempted to strike.

I myself had been in hot water with the Feds for some time,
although it was news to me. Every agency I'd ever heard of (and
some that I was unfamiliar with) had impressive files on Yours
Truly. I was a severely misunderstood individual.

José, Robert and Jim showed up, impersonating reporters,

---

*One of Flash's favorite expressions.

but they were intensely inebriated and their act was not real convincing. Especially José's. He spoke no English and was still wearing his Bandito Outfit, including sombrero and criss-crossed bandoliers. (At this time José was still technically a Full-Blown Dope Lord, but he always had the down-to-earth *attitude* of a Bandito.)

We were being held in a very small jail in a very small town. The details of our escape are unimportant. Suffice it to say that a mixture of tequila, hand grenades and Robert was involved.

We found Harry and the Lear waiting at a local airport, flattened the tires on the squadron of federal, state, local and military aircraft that had arrived after we were apprehended, then hightailed it to the Big Apple. Our rented truck had already left (we'd hired one of Flash's buddies to drive it) and would meet us at our distributor's warehouse in Brooklyn.

We found our boy at his usual blackjack table at an Upper East Side after-hours club at about 6 A.M. Captain C.O.D. is the second-most unbalanced of all my associates, but he doesn't make me anywhere near as nervous as Flash does. For one thing the Captain never travels at high speeds in unsafe vehicles, unless you consider his mind an unsafe vehicle.

Captain C.O.D. is a good old boy from Georgia with a thick backwoods accent and a huge potbelly. His exploits in the marijuana trade are legendary, and he has what can only be described as stupendous connections. His associates run the gamut from Colombian Dope Lords to ex-CIA Cubans to current CIA big shots to down-and-out street hustlers and so on. Everybody likes the Captain.

At any rate, we hadn't seen him in quite some time, so our reunion turned into one of his major productions.

The details of this production are unimportant but it suffices to say that they involved a truck full of marijuana, four limousines, two helicopters, one Learjet, three wholesale liquor outlets, suites at the Sherry Netherlands in New York City and the Queen Elizabeth in Montreal and a cornucopia of Bimbos, Sleazoids and Full-Blown Degenerates, not to mention Captain C.O.D., the Comedy Team from Hell, Flash, Aileron, High Pockets, José and Yours Truly.

The true story of quantum mechanics [is] a truth far stranger than any fiction.   —John Gribbin

Quantum Banditos

The theory of relativity is laughably lightweight stuff compared to Quantum Mechanics and Subatomic Particle Theory in general. I mentioned this to Tina's father in my last volley of Bandito-Mailed Notes, but he has been strangely reticent. I hope and pray that his silence is some sort of Zenlike comment on the Natural Order of Things. The only other explanation is that (as with Quarks) he has become skeptical about my actual existence as a bona fide aspect of reality.

I think it vital at this point to reveal that I believe in Quarks. For those few of you who haven't already done some research on your own, I will give a quick layman's definition of a Quark: A Quark is the most likely candidate at present for the Ultimate Building Block of the Universe.

No one has yet found a Quark, but many are looking. Those scientists who doubt the existence of Quarks are, in my opinion, extremely shortsighted. As proof of this, let us all participate in what Einstein calls a "thought experiment." This is an experiment whose premises are scientifically and logically sound but, for technical reasons, cannot be carried out physically. (Einstein's famous "elevator in vacuum" is a good example.) Since the following experiment is basically *conceptual* in nature, I will dub it "a metaphorical thought experiment." (By the way, I have already tried this experiment with José, and the results were as I had predicted.) Here it is:

Tina's father has never seen me. (I am a metaphorical Quark.) The only evidence he has to confirm my existence is, of course, the notes I wrote that were mailed by José and his scattered Bandito Allies. As I've already mentioned, Tina's father, from his position as an observer, must assume that I am in many different Bandito Strongholds at the same time. That is one possibility. (Quarks also seem to have this property.) But this possibility might be unacceptable to Tina's father because of his limited Worldview. The only other possibility is for him to deny my existence altogether (as he seems to have done with Quarks). If he chooses the latter of the two possibilities, then he will have to either ignore or find some other explanation for my notes.*

Tina's father, I fear, is ignoring the evidence for the existence of Quarks and for the existence of Yours Truly. But we (you, kind reader, and I) have more information at our disposal than Tina's father.

We know that I exist. I know that Quarks exist. Someday someone will find a Quark. Tina's father is unlikely to ever find me. So my mission, my goal in life, is to find Tina's father** and confront him with all this.

"You can't get there from here." —Stephen Hawking, when asked what an encounter with a black hole might be like

---

*For the purposes of the experiment, we must assume that there are no Cosmic Banditos out there cooperating with a devious Quark.
**I am also curious to see how Tina, Tom and Gary are doing. (For some reason, I have never been interested in Tina's mother or her sister, Ruth.)

✳ 12 ✳

Quark Soup*

A Quarky Character is one who, as I see it, goes a bit beyond "spooky." The term "spook" refers to someone involved in clandestine activities.

Some spooks are spies for one government or another, or several simultaneously; some run drugs, guns or, as is usually the case, a combination of the above. But the true Quarky Character (I have coined a concept here) is more difficult to define or, for that matter, locate. Subatomic Particles and clandestine operatives have a lot in common. He (or she, though I've met only one Quarky Female) not only plays both sides of the fence, but has no idea what a fence is at all.

George (that's all we ever knew him as) was one such fellow. His diverse close friends and associates have included Bobby

---

*Quark Soup is an expression some cosmologists use to describe the state of the Universe a few billionths of a second after the Big Bang. It was a situation (I hesitate to use the word "time" because it is unclear if time as we know it had "started") wherein the Universe was so dense that there was no room for Subatomic Particles as we know them. The cosmic Soup of the Day was Consommé of Quark.

Vesco, Richard Nixon, General Mohamar Khaddafi, Golda Meir, Poppa Doc Duvalier, J. Edgar Hoover, Idi Amin, plus various fun-loving guys from various organized-crime groups in various countries. And, naturally, Captain C.O.D.

George was a soft-spoken, well-dressed, conservative-looking man. There was a weird look in his eye, however—a look that gave even Robert the shakes.

After Captain C.O.D. coughed up $890,000 for our gold buds in Manhattan, José talked us (we were now stuck with Flash and Aileron) into paying George a visit in order to procure weaponry for his Bandito Army in Colombia. José felt he was falling behind in the Dope Lord Arms Race.

Robert, Jim and I had met George through a certain ex-CIA operative who has recently come to the attention of the media because of some minor faux pas he made as an arms dealer in the Middle East. We had also hung out with George in Fort Lauderdale when he was associated with Kenny Burnstine, the legendary kingpin of the Marijuana Airforce.*

Robert, Jim and I always had disapproved of blatant gun-runners and hard-drug traffickers. We used guns and drugs, sure, but that was our business. George was different. To him, the world was one giant Pac-Man game and George felt that he had unlimited quarters.

George was not only Quarky—he was downright creepy. He was having dinner with a KGB agent when we located him in a posh Manhattan restaurant, although we had no idea of what was going down.

---

*By the way, it appears to me that every clandestine operative in the known Universe knows every other clandestine operative, regardless of his function in spookdom. The relationship between spooks frequently gets extremely convoluted and often downright bizarre. Whose "side" a spook is on usually becomes a laughable concept. For example, Kenny Burnstine was selling arms to the DEA while under indictment by that same agency for his marijuana-related antics.

Unfortunately, the CIA surveillance team that was taking our pictures from across the street figured we were all in on whatever convoluted scheme George had cooked up with the Bolshevik. This didn't do much for our already tarnished image with the authorities.

George was aware that he was under intense government scrutiny and I felt it was a breach of etiquette that he failed to mention it to us.

The shit hit the fan later that night in George's warehouse in Soho. We'd accompanied José on a tour of inspection of George's merchandise.

Even José was impressed by the awesome firepower the Feds let loose on us. But George was prepared for every scenario. We emerged from his escape route via a manhole on Houston Street.

Our group was now at the top of every governmental shit list. Drug smuggling, inciting to riot and attempted murder (the drive-in theater fiasco), illegal entry into the U.S., assaulting federal agents (High Pockets had taken a chunk out of somebody's leg), breaking jail, blowing up a jail, espionage, arms dealing and unsafe operation of a B-29 were just a few of our offenses. As I have said, we were a severely misunderstood group.

We felt that we had worn out our welcome in the Big Apple, so we had the Lear meet us at a suburban airport and headed south.

In modern terminology, we can now say that quarks come in six flavors.
—James S. Trefil

Cosmic Banditos

José has finally seen the light. I coerced him into spending a weeklong sabbatical from his Bandito Business. My shack was the monastery, I was the teacher. After completely absorbing my Worldview, José is a new man. Through meditation, Subatomic Particle Theory and tequila surreptitiously spiked with ground-up peyote buttons, he now sees the folly of his Bandito Ways.

I led José down the Path of Enlightenment gradually. I eased him into the Quantum World by starting at the beginning, with his mugging of Tina's family. I first posed a question. This was it: If we were able to travel backward in time to the Big Bang, what would the odds be that fifteen billion years hence José would find himself at Santa Marta International, mugging a pubescent nymphomaniac and her family? Naturally José was stumped. I then suggested that a Cosmic Bookie would have probably given us some major-league odds, probably infinity to one. At this José's eyes lit up. He asked me how much we'd bet. This forced me to explain that the size of the bet was irrelevant since an infinite number times anything except zero always equals an infinite number. This threw José off onto another tangent. It took a couple more peyote-spiked bottles of tequila to get him back on track. Using metaphors to reason with a Bandito can be risky.

Anyway, I went on to postulate that the probability that a universe like ours* would actualize, given the possibilities that an infinite number of Alternative Universes could just as easily have been created, was about zero. I then dropped the Big Hint: Maybe in some sense this Universe doesn't "exist" any more than the infinite number of Alternative Universes that didn't (it appears to us) actualize.

I then threw José for a loop by suggesting that it's possible that in addition to Rival Banditos on the other side of the mountain, he might also have Bandito Enemies in an infinite number of other Universes!

The astute reader is obviously aware that I was getting way ahead of myself by delving into the Many Worlds Interpretation of Quantum Mechanics right from the get-go, but José is a tough audience, so I wanted to get his attention before his mind wandered or the drugs wore off.

Anyway, the possibility of an infinite number of Full-Blown Banditos wreaking havoc in an infinite number of Alternative Universes got José's adrenalin pumping. He put his Thompson submachine gun on the table and swiveled around so he could cover the front door just in case some Alternative Banditos decided to actualize in our Universe and storm the shack.

This was more or less how Day One ended. High Pockets and I hit the sack, leaving José guarding the door against a surprise attack by Quantum Banditos.

---

*A universe containing Bananas, Banditos, Contrabandistas and Dope Lords.

Day Two was spent recovering from Day One.

Day Three was spent on Relativity Theory.

Day Four on Heisenberg's Uncertainty Principle and the Particle/Wave Duality.

Day Five on an overview of the works of Lorenz, Dirac, Planck, Bohr and Schrödinger.

Day Six was spent mostly in meditation* and in various other forms of stupors.

Day Seven broke clear and crisp. High Pockets and I got up early and began preparing a hearty breakfast. Legs was nowhere in sight—a stroke of luck since it was Wednesday. José had spent the night in a lotus position in the front yard. He was still out there being bombarded by Subatomic Particles, his sombrero pulled down over his eyes and his Thompson in his lap.

Day Seven was the big day, the day I promised José I would drop the Quantum Bombshell. On Day Seven I would probe the very heart of Quantum Theory. I would describe a phenomenon that is absolutely impossible to explain in any classical or "commonsensical" sort of way, a phenomenon that is the basic peculiarity of all Quantum Mechanics—The Double Slit Experiment.**

The Double Slit Experiment was the coup de grace as far as José was concerned. By the end of Day Seven José had himself become a Quantum Bandito, and as a result no longer suffers from Alternative Bandito Paranoia.

Anyway, I had High Pockets revive José and bring him inside. The three of us stuffed our faces with eggs, goat brains, rice and mescal, then after clean-up I had José sit across the table from me. We sat quietly for a few minutes, contemplating

---

*My meditative technique will probably be dealt with later.
**I suggest that those readers who are easily disoriented or suffer from Intellectual Agoraphobia skip this section.

our digestive tracts. High Pockets was stretched out on the bed, presumably doing the same. I then asked José to remove his sombrero and imagine a brigade of Cosmic Banditos attacking an army garrison at the speed of light. Imagine further, I told him, that there was only one way into the garrison and that only one Bandito at a time could fit through the opening. I reminded José that all Cosmic Banditos (metaphorical photons or Subatomic Particles) are identical. There is no way to tell them apart. Also, Cosmic Banditos have the properties of waves as well as those of particles.

I paused for a moment to light a joint. José had a belt of mescal. He said, "Ahh." I exhaled contemplatively, passed him the joint, then continued.

"Let's say that as the Cosmic Banditos pour through the opening in the garrison wall, some, say sixty percent, head for the Generalissimo's headquarters to pump him full of Cosmic Lead. The remaining forty percent head for the jail to free Cosmic Banditos captured in previous assaults."

At this point José interrupted me with some irrelevant tactical criticisms of the assault itself. I agreed with him before reminding him that Cosmic Banditos are really Subatomic Entities and can't be expected to have his insights into guerrilla warfare. Tact is everything when telling a Bandito that he has his head up his ass.

I rambled on. "As I have told you previously, it is in principle impossible to predict the behavior of any single Cosmic Bandito. We can only predict what they will do as a gang, statistically. Now things get very weird."

I glanced down. Legs's head was sticking out of his favorite crack. He was staring malevolently at High Pockets, who, it appeared, had dozed off.

"Let's say for the sake of argument that the first sixty percent of our attackers bolt for the Generalissimo's headquarters.

Remember that we have already established that, *overall,* sixty percent end up doing this. The impossible now happens. All the remaining Cosmic Banditos automatically head for the jail."

I had a belt of mescal and slammed the bottle onto the table for emphasis. "Think about it."

José scratched his three-day growth, nodding sagely.

His eyes lit up momentarily, then dimmed.

He said, "Ahh."

He shook his head.

He fiddled with his sombrero.

Then he admitted that he was stumped and asked how the last forty percent had known that their mission was to storm the jail.

I was very pleased with this response. José was catching on. I dropped the metaphor.

"Now you've gotten to the crux of the matter." I was getting excited so I had a couple more belts of mescal to calm my nerves. "It appears that any given Subatomic Unit *knows* the *Quantum State* of any and all other Subatomic Units in its system!"

José cut loose with the longest "Ahhhhhhhhh" I'd ever heard.

"The conclusion we must come to is inescapable. Denizens of the Subatomic Realm *process information* and they do it instantaneously!"

José stood up and started pacing.

"E.H. Walker has postulated that Subatomic Particles are, in some sense, *conscious entities!*"

I went on to describe what happens when there are two ways into the garrison (hence the name "Double Slit Experiment"). Two slits cause Subatomic Units to "interface" with each other because of their wave-like properties. The astounding result of this aspect of the experiment* is that as Subatomic Units pass through one slit or the other, they "know" whether or not the other slit is open regardless of whether it's being used by other Units. In other words, not only do they know what each other is doing, but they also know the entire experimental setup! The real bombshell—not that these bombshells aren't enough—is that the little bastards actually seem to know when they are being watched and alter their behavior accordingly (and randomly). Subatomic Particles seem to be giving the Universe the Cosmic Finger. "Fuck off," they seem to be saying. "Mind your own business."

At this point High Pockets let out a yelp. I looked over at the bed. Legs had him by the nose and had wrapped his body around High Pockets' neck. High Pockets was howling like a maniac and shaking his head, but it was obvious that Legs had planned his sneak attack perfectly. There was absolutely nothing High Pockets could do.

"Fucking Wednesdays," I muttered as I tried to corral High Pockets, who was now staggering sideways toward the door, yelping and whining. Legs dug his little teeth further into High Pockets' nose and wrapped the tip of his tail around High Pockets' left ear for a better grip.

I wrestled High Pockets to the floor and pinned him. I then grasped Legs just behind the head and pried him loose from High Pockets' nose, which was leaking blood from dozens of tiny holes. I unwrapped Legs's body from High Pockets' neck, lost my balance and somersaulted over backward, ending up in an unnatural position under the table. High Pockets bounded out the door and disappeared into the jungle, still howling in fright and pain. I looked at Legs.

---

*I spent the whole day explaining the Double Slit Experiment to José and have no intention of doing the same for you all. If you want to learn more about the Double Slit Experiment or anything else about the New Physics, I'm sure you'll have an easier time finding research material than I did.

"What the fuck is the matter with you?" I roared. Legs regarded me with his beady little eyes, a bored expression on his face. I stuffed him down the crack and told him not to come back until he'd straightened out his act.

I stood up and dusted myself off. José was still pacing back and forth, mumbling to himself in Spanish.

He gestured for me to sit. I did. I started complaining about Legs' fucking attitude. José motioned for me to be silent, then spoke softly. He said he thought Cosmic Banditos were pretty similar to Real-Life Banditos.

Thus far I hadn't thought much about the metaphors I'd been using as a teaching device. I considered José's statement for a moment, then had an "aha" experience.

"Chemistry, therefore biochemistry, is closely dependent on Quantum Theory," I mused. "Maybe the relationship extends itself." I paused. "Maybe even to the world as we know it. The world of Bananas, Banditos, Contrabandistas and Dope Lords."

"*Exactamente*," José said. Without another word he walked slowly out of the shack, mounted Pepe and disappeared into the jungle.

He didn't show up again until yesterday.

He explained that he now fully understands my situation with respect to Tina's father and insisted on accompanying High Pockets and me on our pilgrimage to Sausalito.

Because of our problems with the authorities (fools that they are), it will be a long, dangerous journey, but José and I believe that destiny is on our side. We will make our way under cover of darkness, as it were, from one Bandito Stronghold to the next, gaining aid and succor from José's Bandito Allies. We will make our way north, through Central America to Mexico, where we will enter the United States by bolting across the border with the first group of wetbacks we can locate.

Then north, ever north to Sausalito. And Tina's father.

José, Noble Savage that he is, concocted a concept that I find mind-boggling in its brilliance and simplicity. (The true scientist's Worldview is childlike.) I call his plan the Concept of the Creeping Banditos. Here it is: The pattern of my note-sending will change from the Simultaneous Bandito Stronghold Theory to the Encroaching Bandito Theory. I am certain that Tina's father has a map of South and Central America with little pins and dates on it, each pin representing a Bandito Stronghold that it appeared I mailed a message from. With José and me sending messages from each Bandito Stronghold as we move north, it will soon become obvious to Tina's father that we are *creeping up on him!* As we close in, the messages themselves will become progressively more cryptic and abstract. We'll keep a sharp eye on the *International Trib*'s classified ads to see his reaction.

I think Tina's father will get the idea when I start slipping in references to Gravitational Theory. I'm sure he will understand the metaphor.

The mutual attraction of two celestial bodies is inversely proportional to the square of the distance between them. —Albert Einstein

✳ 14 ✳

The Earth Sucks*

I've always maintained that the best way to see New York City is from the back of an outbound Learjet at 46,000 feet.

It was pretty crowded and somewhat rowdy in the back. Harry, as usual, had amply stocked the jet with bubbly and exotic snacks. High Pockets' favorite was goose liver pâté with a dollop of black Russian caviar on top. Aileron, like Flash, was indiscriminate in his culinary habits. The rest of us—José, Jim, Robert and myself—mostly concentrated on the champagne and on planning our next move.

Harry stuck his head into the cabin and inquired about a possible destination. Everyone yelled out a different suggestion, so I told him we'd get back to him.

At this point, Flash got it into his head that he wanted to try his hand at the controls, having never flown a high-

---

*A vital aspect of Flash's Theory of Gravitation.

powered bullet like the Learjet. Harry said, "Sure." This turned out to be a mistake.

Since we didn't know where we were going, Flash thought he'd practice some aerobatic maneuvers. This didn't bother anybody (we were used to spilt champagne in the back) but it had unseen repercussions far below on the ground.

The Feds (a veritable army of them by now) had alerted all the air-traffic controllers in the Northeast to report any erratically-flying aircraft. Any aircraft that seemed to by flying *aimlessly* (a perfect description of our behavior on every level— aimless). The cops had finally figured us out. It had always been nearly impossible to keep track of us because there was no pattern to our criminal activities. Since *we* never really knew what we were doing, how could anyone else?*

Flash's bizarre flight path, the obvious lack of intelligent thought behind his random arcs and sweeps in the strato- sphere, was immediately seen on every radar screen in at least six states. The die was cast. The authorities were mobilized. They would track us wherever we went. What goes up must come down—and when we did, they'd be waiting.

I dimly recall the plan we hatched while we rolled and looped over the mid-Atlantic states.

The first order of business was to do some serious partying. Since none of us lived anywhere in particular, we had to come up with a host who would put up with us for a week or so. In short, a host with the correct *attitude*. Someone who perceived chaos and destruction as not only acceptable but inevitable.

Our list of possible party-throwers was quite long, but we

---

*This is a good example of Heisenberg's Uncertainty Principle, a cornerstone of Quantum Theory. The Uncertainty Principle states that one can know the position of a Subatomic Particle *or* its momentum, but never both simultane- ously. In other words, a randomly moving target is hard to hit.

settled on Eduardo, still in exile in Miami. His status as former Dope Lord and José's cousin made him the sentimental favorite.

My recollection of the remainder of our misguided, protracted endeavors is very hazy. I believe someone suggested we buy a freighter of some sort. I vaguely recall José mentioning the sister ship of the long-lost *Don Juan*. I suspect that I passed out during the discussion, because the next thing I remember is our landing in Homestead, just outside Miami.

It is impossible to get anywhere without sinning against reason.
—Albert Einstein

✳ 15 ✳

Zen Banditos

The sun has just set over a small lake near the Nicaraguan border. High Pockets, José and I are camped on the eastern shore with a bunch of Left-Wing Banditos. It was a rough three weeks getting here. There will be no campfire tonight. We shot up some government troops earlier in the day and can't risk being spotted.

José and I have been trying to reason with these Politically Bent Banditos, as we have with all the Banditos we've been hanging out with during our trip. Reasoning with Banditos is tough, and I'm no miracle worker. A day or so with each band just isn't enough, but José and I have been doing our best as Missionaries of Bandito Enlightenment. We have brought as many books as Pepe, our little burro, can carry, and José is making great progress in his continuing Quest for Knowledge. Each night we sit down for an hour or so of intensive study. Since José can't read, I'm his instructor. He is an excellent student, although his mind occasionally wanders. Fond recollections of his Bandito Past, I suspect. But he has more or less mastered Subatomic Particle Theory and we are now delving into Astrophysics.*

José's Bandito Reputation has preceded him everywhere, so we always get a rousing welcome, but some Banditos get sullen when we try to change their Bandito Worldviews. I find these Left-Wing Banditos particularly exasperating. They always seem to be in a bad mood (a sure sign that something's lacking in Marxist philosophy). Most Banditos have no interest in the New Physics, especially when they're cranky, but we've made converts here and there. Mostly in Costa Rica, where the Banditos are more happy-go-lucky. Someday I will return there and set up a Bandito School of Physics and Cosmology. If the idea catches on, it could bring peace to this troubled part of the world. As Banditos learn the Underlying Nature of Reality, they will throw down their weapons. I am certain of that.**

In fact, the one major success we've had was in Costa Rica, and it was more or less accidental. We stumbled across a Bandito Stronghold that José was unfamiliar with. As a matter of fact, it was a temporary, ad hoc sort of Bandito Stronghold that consisted of a dozen or so tents pitched by a small stream in a beautiful, lush valley that had once been part of a banana plantation.

We were making our way along the bank of the stream when José, walking point with High Pockets, froze. I looked

---

*The astute reader is obviously aware that I occasionally make references to the Macrocosmic Realm (Cosmology, Gravitational Theory, Astrophysics, etc.). The reason is simple: The division between the Microcosmic and the Macrocosmic is probably an illusory one, a result of the propensity of the human mind to categorize phenomena. José and I both believe that someday a Grand Unified Theory (GUT) will emerge to explain all observable events, whether they are Quantum or Cosmological. Even if this Unification is never achieved (some scientists believe it impossible even in principle), José and I like to think of ourselves as Well-Rounded Guys (WRGs) so we are making a concerted effort to keep our Pulses on the Finger of Reality.
**José and I have already adopted a pacifistic outlook but we are always heavily armed, just in case.

around: Several dozen Banditos had appeared out of nowhere and had us covered with a motley array of weapons, including a young Budding Bandito with a BB gun.

There were some tense moments as they escorted us to their camp, first taking our weapons and fitting High Pockets with a makeshift muzzle.

Everything turned out to be okay, however. The gang's leader, a Full-Blown Bandito named Fredi, turned out to be a distant relative of José's. Once this was established, we were treated with the utmost respect and courtesy. We were bathed by Bandito Maidens, fed and given all the mescal we wanted. Pepe was also fed and watered and High Pockets was given his choice of the many Bandito Bitches (all True Banditos like dogs) that were scratching around the camp.*

Fredi declared a holiday from Bandito Business and had his men prepare a fiesta in our honor.

As night fell, cooking fires and torches were lit, a few pigs were slaughtered and roasted and gallons of mescal were broken out. Another score of Banditos from nearby strongholds also showed up, having heard of our arrival through the Bandito Grapevine.

Meanwhile, José and I conspired in private as to what tack we would take with this group, by far the largest number of Banditos we'd run into since embarking on our Quest. José persuaded me to let him handle things this time since my track record as Professor of Bandito Physics had, so far, been dismal. I told him to give it a shot. His results were spectacular, I have to admit.

As we sat down to dinner, Fredi mentioned that he'd heard

---

*He chose a big shaggy bitch with as questionable a genetic heritage as his own and disappeared into the jungle. The two emerged about an hour later looking very pleased with themselves. We will try to return in a few months to see what sort of bizarre offspring might have resulted.

José had had some problems back in Colombia and offered to help out in any way he could.

This was the opening José had been waiting for. He casually asked Fredi if it would be okay to address the camp, whose ranks had swollen to about sixty, after dinner.

Fredi agreed immediately, then bellowed for more mescal, which, following José's orders, I had spiked with copious quantities of psylisibic mushrooms.

The fiesta turned out to be your basic Bandito Bash: huge amounts of food and mescal, a lot of raucous laughter and Bandito Braggadocio, a few fistfights and, of course, an improvised fireworks display consisting of mortar and rocket launcher fire. The finale was supplied by a Pyromaniacal Bandito with a flamethrower.*

José kept asking me what time it was. I knew what he was doing: calculating when the psylicibin would be kicking in. I didn't need a watch to figure this out: I was blasted out of my gourd.

José's plan to get the Banditos psychedelically plastered before his lecture was a brilliant one, but what he did next was the masterstroke and I felt some sort of cross-eyed embarrassment for not having thought of it myself.

First, a digression is necessary. Traveling back in time to Chapter 13, the reader might recall that part of José's conversion from a simple (though not to be taken lightly) Bandito to a Subatomic Bandito involved meditation. At that time I promised you all would eventually hear about my technique. Well, "eventually" then is the present now.**

I devised this meditative technique while High Pockets

---

*I've never cared for Bandito Fireworks Displays, by the way. Neither mortars nor rocket launchers were meant to be shot straight up, for obvious reasons.
**We will eventually delve more extensively into the concept of time travel. At *that* time the "eventually" of the here and now will have eventualized.

and I were living alone back at the shack, soon after the mugging of Tina's Family and its effects on my Worldview. It seems like a lifetime ago.

Most types of meditation involve some sort of bullshit mantra, usually an inane word some towel-headed moron gives you after you cough up a few bucks.

Well, my mantra isn't inane and it won't cost you anything (assuming you either borrowed or stole this book).

When I was a kid I went to summer camp.* It was about a four-hour ride to the camp and the bus was always packed with dozens of future Barristers, Bankers, and other Banditos-To-Be.

Anyway, there was this sap who had to accompany us on the trip. His job was to keep chaos and destruction to a minimum.

One method always worked, and looking back on it now, I realize why. Remember "Row, Row, Row Your Boat?" Well, that's it. That's my mantra.

> *Row, row, row your boat*
> *Gently down the stream.*
> *Merrily, merrily, merrily, merrily*
> *Life is but a dream.*

Talk about a Subatomic Tune! Think about it.** If you don't believe there are some major-league metaphors going on here, I suggest you put this book down and forget it. Go read some Kahlil Gibran.

---

*Believe it or not, I had a normal childhood. I can't for the life of me fathom how I turned out this way.
**If you think any kid's song will work just as well, try meditating to "One Hundred Bottles of Beer on the Wall." You'll end up on a college steeple with a rifle.

Life is but a dream. *

Jesus Christ, no wonder it calmed us down. What's the point of destroying a bus or punching some other little prick's lights out if the whole mess is just a fucking dream?

Anyway, I ran into a hitch up at the shack. This method of transcendental meditation works best if you do it in harmony (a three-part harmony is the best). I suspect this has something to do with certain harmonic properties (illusory as they may be) of the Macrocosmic World.

Obviously, I had no one to harmonize with. Or so I thought. The second time I tried my mantra, High Pockets was sitting next to me. You guessed it. He started howling or, more accurately, wailing in harmony, as only a big mutt with a depraved puppyhood can wail.

This worked out fairly well until José's conversion, which afforded me a three-part harmony. The profundity of some of my experiences while under the influence of a Row-Row-Row-Your-Boat High are impossible to convey on paper. Suffice to say that both José and I agree it has put us in closer touch with the Subatomic World. José even claims he has formed an alliance with an Alternative Bandito from the O-Zone. God only knows what kind of weird doggy trips High Pockets has been taking.

Anyway, José separated the sixty Blasted Banditos into three sections. He had them form a circle around a blazing bonfire, tenors to the north, altos to the east and baritones to the south. José stood on the west side of the campfire and called out for silence.

---

*Scientists hesitate to use the word "dream" when describing the Nature of Reality, but they keep running off at the mouth with statements like "We conjure up the universe," "We are participators in reality" and "Reality is essentially nonsubstantial." Sounds like a dream to me, Jackson.

I sat a few yards behind him in case he needed coaching.

High Pockets had gone back into the jungle with his little Canine Cupcake to knock off another piece.

José paced back and forth in front of the three-score Silent Banditos for a minute or so, gathering his thoughts and having an occasional belt of mescal.

José knew Banditos don't normally sit around the campfire singing "Row, Row, Row Your Boat," so he first softened them up by complimenting everything about them, from their excellent Bandito Cuisine to their oversize Bandito Sombreros. Between the psychedelic mushrooms and a few minutes of this bullshit, José had them eating out of his hand.

He then asked if everybody trusted him. A chorus of "*Sí Sí's*," "*Naturalmentes*" and "*Seguro hombres.*"

About a half hour later, José had taught the group "Row, Row, Row Your Boat" in English—it doesn't have the same effect in Spanish, probably because it doesn't rhyme—and explained what the words meant. (Incidentally, "Row, Row, Row Your Boat" is the only English José knows.) He rehearsed each of the three sections separately, then held up his now empty mescal bottle like a conductor's baton.

"*Uno, dos, tres, quatro.*" And the chorus began, softly at first, then a little louder, then louder still, until the jungle reverberated with a joyously whacked-out Bandito Choir singing in perfect three-part harmony.

High Pockets and his girlfriend were howling from somewhere in the jungle.

Stars twinkled overhead.

Pulsars pulsed.

Quasars quased.

Subatomic Particles bombarded the earth and all its children.

Goose bumps erupted all over my body.

Suddenly José waved his bottle for the chorus to stop.

The ensuing quiet was a truly Cosmic Silence. In front of José lay a silent sea of motionless sombreros.

The thought crossed my mind that if José's Bandito Audience was even half as whacked as I was, he was going to have one helluva successful lecture. That is, if he could keep *his* head together.

As it turned out, José not only kept his head together, but also gave probably the most insightful discourse on the Underlying Nature of Reality any Bandito has ever heard.

Naturally, he started at the beginning, with his mugging of Tina's family. In order to avoid any Bandito Outbursts, he skirted the issue of Tina's betrayal of Tom and Gary, making only brief mention of her nymphomania (and, of course, not a hint about the concealed diaphragm).

He then shocked the hell out of me by immediately reviewing the Double Slit Experiment and its implications vis à vis Bandito Consciousness, both Cosmic and Real-Life. A Bandito in the back of the tenor section punctuated José's summation of this concept by firing a mortar shell more or less straight up. It eventually came down about fifty yards away in the jungle. Dirt, debris and pureed bananas rained down on the camp, but José continued without missing a beat.

He spent the next hour or so reviewing Quantum Theory in general. José's teaching methods differed from mine in one vital aspect: He never brought up Newton or any of the other old farts that predated the New Physics, and, in retrospect, I have to agree with his reasoning. Why confuse the issue with irrelevant theories?

His Bandito Audience sat rapt and quiet—except for that one Bandito Tenor who kept launching mortar rounds in response to José's more mind-expanding utterances.

As he began to delve into the problem of Schrödinger's

Bandito, however, a volley of randomly aimed rocket launcher fire erupted from the baritone section. The scene was starting to get downright surreal.*

José did a brilliant segue into a Full-Blown Discourse on the nature of Space, Time and Matter. I drained the remainder of my mescal and smiled at my protégé's insights like a proud father.

José paced back and forth, occasionally gesturing with his bottle as he explained that the world as we know it, the world of Bananas and Banditos (I assumed he'd left out Contra-bandistas and Dope Lords for the sake of brevity), is merely an image formed by standing and moving waves of electro-magnetism and Subatomic Processes, and how the findings of Quantum Mechanics have virtually destroyed the notion of "solid" objects.

At this point, a solid object landed directly in front of José. The object turned out to be a mortar shell. For some reason, it was a dud.

José gave it a quick glance and rambled on. I could tell he was getting a little disoriented from the way he lapsed in and out of metaphors. First he would call an electron an electron, then he would refer to it as a Cosmic Bandito.** He was still basically coherent, however, and went on to explain that as a direct result of Heisenberg's Uncertainty Principle, electrons are sometimes seen to be spread over a wide area and some-times localized in a small region. Moreover, just when we feel we have a Cosmic Bandito's location pinpointed, it might fool us and be somewhere else.

At this point High Pockets appeared and lay down with his

---

*By this time I was actively hallucinating, so my perceptions of the remain-der of the lecture should be taken with a grain or so of salt.
**Perhaps this Electron/Cosmic Bandito duality is analogous to the particle/wave duality of Subatomic Units.

head on my lap. He was visibly shaken by the sporadic and indiscriminate mortar, rocket launcher and small-arms fire coming from the Bandito Chorus. I fumbled through my pockets and came up with our last Milk Bone Flavor Snack for Small Dogs, but he was too upset to eat. He also seemed exhausted, probably from his girlfriend's sexual demands.

I looked at José. He was swilling mescal from a fresh bottle. After a particularly healthy pull, he wiped his mouth with his sleeve, said, "Ahh," doffed his sombrero and warned his audience he was about to explain the Real Underlying Nature of Reality. He asked the Banditos if they were ready.

The mob answered with a fresh volley of heavenward-aimed projectiles.*

José then began a slurred dissertation on one of the most difficult concepts of the New Physics: The concept of the Curvature of Space. The Bandito Barrage eased up and then stopped altogether (except for an occasional shot from the jerk in the back of the tenor section) as José explained the nature of the Space-Time Continuum. Time, he asserted, is not a separate entity from three-dimensional space but a part of the same something, and that there is no universal flow of time, any more than there is a universal flow of upwardness or downwardness.

Moreover, he continued, the very fabric of space-time is not straight, as everyday experience leads us to believe, but curved.

A pregnant pause. José had a slug of mescal, then belched contemplatively. He had his audience by the short hairs and he knew it.

---

*My cranial nerve synapses were now firing randomly but I did sense some sort of balance between upwardly shot Bandito Projectiles and downwardly zipping Subatomic Particles.

This curvature, José asserted, manifests itself in such phenomena as gravity. And, he hinted, possibly matter itself.

Another pregnant pause.

I was dumbstruck by the timing and profundity of José's delivery. He then quoted (in Spanish, of course) one of his favorite modern-day physicists, John Wheeler: "There is nothing in the world except empty, curved space. Matter, charge, electromagnetism and other fields are only manifestations of the bending of space. *Physics is geometry*."

José jabbed the Space-Time Continuum with his mescal bottle. Bananas and Banditos, he asserted, are mere undulations of nothingness!

This statement precipitated another spontaneous eruption of small-arms fire. Several mortar rounds exploded nearby, showering José's Bandito Symposium with more debris.

José removed a shredded banana peel from his face and bellowed for silence.

He looked up at the stars, seeking inspiration, then ordered the mob to remove their sombreros and do likewise.

The sight of three-score Banditos silently staring into the Cosmos made me dizzy, so I looked down at High Pockets and stroked his head. His tail, as usual, wagged.

"The Great Spirit wags," I mumbled, briefly thinking of the old Indian, wherever he was. I then thought of Señor Rodriguez, Tina, Tom, Gary and, especially, Tina's father.

This resulted in my slipping into a reverie. Possibly it was a coma of some sort.

Anyway, when my mind returned from vacation José was well into a dissertation on our favorite subject: The Many Worlds Interpretation of Quantum Mechanics. He reviewed the concepts of Collapsing Wave Functions, Ghost Particles,

Antimatter and Tina's father. He then turned his attention to the Editions Theory of the Interpretation. I could hear the idiot in the tenor section yelling for more mortar shells.

A Bandito in the alto section fired a short burst from what sounded like an Uzi. I sensed the mob was starting to get excited.

When José boasted that he had formed an alliance with an Alternative Full-Blown Bandito from another Branch of Reality, the crowd went wild. The Bandito Chorus discharged whatever weapons they were holding simultaneously.

High Pockets jumped about ten feet straight up.

José was knocked flat on his back by the shock wave.

The maniac with the flamethrower shot a fountain of fire across the camp.

The sky and surrounding jungle lit up in orange and blue.

Ripe and semiripe bananas rained down from the heavens.

A hand grenade rolled into the ammunition tent and went off.

I was struck by flying debris and lost consciousness.

All in all, I have to rate José's lecture an unqualified success.

Two nights ago, however, he tried to duplicate this success with a band of Marxist Banditos in southern Nicaragua. Unfortunately, this lecture didn't go very well. In retrospect, I have more or less figured out why. First of all, I hesitate to categorize the gang as True Banditos. They wore olive-drab fatigues instead of the prescribed buckskin-and-leather Bandito Outfits. They didn't care for dogs either, always a bad sign. On the other hand, I don't want to appear snobbish on this matter, so I'll give the assholes the benefit of the doubt.

José's problems with these guys started right at the get-go. First they refused to drink the mushroom-laced mescal I offered them, claiming they had to get up early and wanted to be clear-headed for some sort of ambush.*

They also refused José's invitation to sing "Row, Row, Row Your Boat" for fear of being detected by government troops or the CIA.

The shit hit the fan about two minutes into José's lecture on Basic Bandito Physics 101. Someone in the back yelled for José to shut up so he could get some sleep. The rest of the crew agreed vociferously. One guy made the mistake of tossing a half-eaten plantain at José.

High Pockets and I saw it coming and dove for cover.

José acquitted himself quite well, even though he was severely outnumbered. He wound up with two black eyes, another lump on the forehead and his gold front tooth knocked out (he found it in the morning), but the only real damage was to his Bandito Pride.**

José had been of great help to me in my message-writing to Tina's father (and to Tom, Gary and Tina). He has a real flair for the abstract. Once in a while I let him dictate a note in its entirety, correcting only his bad Bandito Grammar.

We have been checking the classified ads in the *International Trib* whenever we can get a copy, but Tina's father has been silent. I suspect we'll hear from him as our inexorable northward progress becomes unmistakable. When he realizes that like Newton's apple plummeting to Earth we are on an almost *gravitational* mission, he will have little choice.

José and I (not to mention High Pockets) are arrows in

---

*I've never met a Bandito who felt he had to be clearheaded for anything, but I'm even willing to let this piece of Anti-Bandito Behavior slide.

**I have resigned myself to the fact that José was, is and always will be a Bandito. The philosophy behind his Bandito Behavior has increased in profundity, however.

flight—conceptual arrows, shot from the bow of the Ultimate Zen Archer.* Arrows arching through the Space-Time Continuum. Arrows aimed directly at the Worldview of Tina's father.

Quantum Mechanics can be seen as a rediscovery of Shiva, the Hindu god of chaos and destruction. —Gary Zukav

---

*By the way, Eastern Philosophy (particularly Zen Buddhism) and the New Physics appear to have come to some of the same conclusions from two very different directions.

✳ 16 ✳

The Sad Bandito

We called Eduardo in Miami via the Lear's skyphone and had a ridiculous, rambling conversation with him about old times and the upcoming party. Naturally, approximately 18,000 Feds were listening in. Ten minutes after we hung up, Eduardo's house was overrun by a DEA SWAT Team. Next, the Feds amassed several hundred undercover agents in three-piece suits at the almost-deserted General Aviation Terminal at Miami International and told them to look casual. This was a mistake.

It is a known fact that General Aviation (the private aircraft industry) in South Florida is heavily dependent on drug traffickers to keep its planes in the air; and since we're the happy-go-luckiest of tippers, when it comes down to a popularity poll between your basic Contrabandista with his foolish grin and pocketful of hundreds and the forces of all that's right and good, I'm afraid the bad guys get the nod as far as most folks go.*

---

*The situation is exactly the same with respect to yacht and ship brokers, marine parts manufacturers, marina personnel, etc. They're all in on it.

Flash kept us at about 100 feet, roaring between buildings in downtown Miami Beach, then out over the water, turning south toward the blue Caribbean.

Things were not looking good. The Lear would be confiscated, along with the $890,000 in the back (or whatever was left after the Feds divided it up amongst themselves). My two best friends were in jail. A serious jail, not some outhouse with a bicycle lock in Massachusetts.

The three of us owned an offshore corporation in the Cayman Islands with a couple million or so left in it, but it took two of us to draw money out. We had set it up as sort of a joke when we were seriously wealthy a few years back. I couldn't even remember the name of the bank, never mind the corporation. With both Robert and Jim in limbo, that money was gone, too.

I tallied my assets. Not including loose change, I had $312.

José said not to worry. We'd go back to Riohacha, collect his Bandito Army, smuggle them back to the States, storm whatever jail they had the boys in, then get back down to normal business. It sounded good to me, but unfortunately things didn't go exactly as we planned.

The first thing was that Flash missed South America. Just before dawn, we crossed Central America somewhere south of the Canal without realizing it. Flash continued to wing his way south, but he was over the *Pacific*, not the Caribbean. I had taken a nap and crawled back into the copilot's seat at about 0800. I calculated that we should've been on the ground in Colombia by then. Ahead was nothing but ocean.

Flash's explanation was "headwinds."

When I inquired about the snowcapped mountains fifty or so miles off on our left side, he told me to leave him alone.

"There shouldn't be anything out that way until Africa," I said.

"Then it's Africa," he replied.

"You have no idea where we are," I said.

A contemplative pause. Flash fired up one of his Rastafumian Bombers and exhaled. "Look," he said. "I know exactly where we are. We're right *here*." He pointed down. "It's everyplace else that I've got some problems with."

We finally hung a left and landed at a little coastal strip in Bolivia for directions. While we were being refueled and redirected, I bought a local newspaper. My picture was plastered across the front page. There was a smaller picture, an insert, of High Pockets, his tongue hanging out foolishly. I suddenly felt dizzy, disoriented. What were High Pockets and I doing in a local Bolivian newspaper? We had broken a few laws here in the past, but nothing very serious. I quickly skimmed through the story.

I was now a left-wing terrorist and had been seen recently in the company of the infamous Carlos. My mission, the story said, was to assassinate every president and dictator in the Third World. High Pockets, they claimed, was a Canine Killing Machine. We had both been trained in Libya by our old friend "known only as 'George'" and were able, through specially developed meditative techniques, to blow ourselves up by force of will.

We were numero uno on the hit parade of every agency of every government represented in the United Nations (and a few that weren't).

"This is outright slander," I mumbled to High Pockets, not realizing that he had wandered off. I tried to figure out who or what had caused this gross misinterpretation. They had mentioned George. That was a clue. I thought of Robert and Jim, wherever they were. Those two idiots would say anything for a laugh, especially when they were high and under interrogation. But this story was too coherent.

I turned the page absently. To my surprise, *José's* picture was plastered across *that*. This was getting ridiculous. I started reading. "Oh, boy," was one of the things I said before finishing. I looked up. José was sitting in the dirt eating a Bolivian Burrito with a Bolivian Bandito. I suddenly needed a drink. There was bad news here for José, too. Here it is: Because of José's "ties" to me, George and Carlos the Terrorist, he had been linked to a Marxist Revolutionary Front in Colombia. Apparently his Dope Lord Cronies got wind of this in Riohacha and ran amok with José's Empire. Communism is the biggest no-no of all in the Dope Lord Code of Conduct.*

According to a Dope Lord spokesman, José's Bandito Army defected to various other Dope Lord Armies, with only a handful of his most loyal men fleeing to the southwest to await his return.

I got up slowly and looked around.

High Pockets and Aileron were sniffing Bolivian doggy behinds near a couple thatched huts.

Flash was supervising the Lodestar's refueling by peering into the tank with a lit joint in his mouth.

José was picking a flea or louse from his three-day growth and nodding sagely while the other Bandito filled him in on the local Bandito Gossip. Apparently the guy hadn't heard about José's problems.

There was a small, corrugated-metal general store a few yards away, so I walked over and in. The only things they sold were flour, tequila and STP fuel additive. I bought three bottles of tequila and went back outside, still a little woozy from what I'd read.

---

*By the way, no one knows who the first Dope Lord was, but according to recent Dope Lord Archaeological finds he predated Moses by some 900 years.

I took a long pull of tequila,* gagged slightly, straightened up and made my way over to where José and his buddy sat in the shade of a gnarled old oak, the only tree for a mile or so along the wild coastline. I sat down.

I handed each Bandito a bottle, then took another serious swallow. In fact, I drained half the bottle. My lips stretched across my teeth involuntarily and I could feel blood being diverted toward my eyeballs in case they decided to get bloodshot.

"Aaee-aah!" I yelled. This also was involuntary, but the two Banditos took it as a challenge and proceeded to chug-a-lug their bottles.

"Ahhh . . ." José said.

"Ahhh . . ." José's buddy said.

This was more or less what I'd hoped would happen. I looked at my watch. I'd give José's system five minutes to get the tequila pumping, then tell him about his empire having been pillaged and all. First I would read him the front-page article about me to get him laughing. Timing is everything when breaking bad news to a Bandito.

I waited the five minutes, during which time José got three more bottles of tequila. (I still hadn't finished my first.) He and his buddy chug-a-lugged theirs again. Again they both said, "Ahh . . ." I started the story.

José listened attentively, laughed at my part, then looked at his own picture on the second page. He puffed up like a rawhide-and-buckskin canary. He deflated slowly, like a leaky balloon, however, as I read on. From his eyes I couldn't tell whether he was just extremely drunk or Out-of-Control Bandito Drunk, which is like the hyperspace of drunkdom.

---

*Banditos don't use salt or lime, by the way. They have an old saying about people that do use them, but I can't for the life of me remember it.

In point of fact, neither was the case, which is one of the many reasons I will always respect José as a leader of men. The effect of the bad news on him was this and only this: It sobered him up.

He calmly asked his Bandito Buddy where the nearest phone was. The guy said about an hour or so to the south by jeep. José then told me he'd be back in a couple hours or so, and left with the guy after negotiating for the use of the town's only jeep.

I was passed out under the tree when he got back. He sat down and woke me gently. José was a Sad Bandito.* Everything was true. He couldn't return to Riohacha until he'd reconsolidated himself and defeated the Dope Lord who'd stabbed him in the back, using José's nonexistent leftist leanings to foment dissent amongst his men. José had twenty good men, though, camped in the Sierra Nevadas.

He had other news. About me. There were bounties on High Pockets and me from various dictators (plus the CIA) that added up to over $200,000. No one could be trusted. The whole continent was crawling with agents, double agents and informers.

José gave me one of his special Bandito Embraces and told me not to worry. He'd take care of me until we got back on our feet.

We passed another bottle of tequila between us. José called Flash over and had me explain things. José (through me) then told Flash he was welcome to come up and hide out with us. He further explained that the Lodestar was hot as a jalapeño

---

*He now truly *was* a Bandito, having lost his status as Dope Lord, but, as I have said, José was so down-to-earth a guy that he acted like a Bandito even when he was a Dope Lord.

and was therefore unsafe for travel. José and I would be continuing on by jeep and, later, by burro.

Flash fiddled with his crimson ponytail and smiled. "Thanks, maan, but me and old Aileron, we're used to livin' in a plane, ya know?" He slipped the rubberband back over his ponytail and rambled on. "Ya know, this is an even nicer set of wings than the old *Looney Tune* and, man, when I finish customizing this dude with the old red, white and blue Flasheroo paint job, ya know, who's going to recognize the sucker?"

Flash started to walk back to the plane. He turned suddenly. "Treetop level, man. Very important concept."

He then pointed at me, though he spoke to José. "This dude is *heavy*, man. His *mind* is at treetop level."

With that, Flash and Aileron boarded the Lodestar (he had already started calling her the "Loaded Star"), cranked her up and took off.

Three weeks later José and I reached his men in the mountains south of Santa Marta. High Pockets and I moved into our shack and this tale began. Or the tale behind this tale began, since this part was the part of the tale that dealt with how the tale got into position where it mattered how it began at all.

When I first started to write this story I had it in my mind that it would end when the past caught up with the present (as it now has done), but things didn't work out exactly as I planned. Something has happened here that seems to happen all too often in life itself: *The present has gotten out of hand.* I'll tell you something. If I ever write another book (very doubtful) I'll do the whole goddamn thing in the past tense, so at least I'll know what will get out of hand before I start.

Hey, I have a quick conceptual quiz for you all. Here it is: The past and present sections of this story have now converged on each other.* There are two possibilities that can explain this. Either the present part of the story slowed down a bit and waited for the past part to catch up, or the past part speeded up and overtook the present part. (We will overlook other possible combinations of these two possibilities.) Which of the above two possibilities has actualized? I'll give you a minute to think.

Ready?

The answer is this: If your body didn't eject gas or air in a scornful, involuntary eruption (a laugh followed by a fart would've been the best reaction), you failed miserably.

From a relativistic standpoint (and there probably is no other standpoint), my question is meaningless. I meant it comedically for those of you who have done your homework.

The question is also meaningless in the sense that the present cannot slow down and wait, either in a narrative or in life. It just rambles on like the village idiot.

Let me add at this point that if you haven't as yet taken it upon yourself to do some outside research, I would prefer that

---

*Mainly the characters, past and present. Take José, High Pockets and me. As our pasts and presents converged, we could have run into ourselves—in the jungle, let's say. High Pockets (both of him) would've hightailed it for the shack and run into each other again under my bed, then they would've both freaked out again and gone to some other identical place. And so on, ad infinitum. José (both of him) would've shot himself on the spot, leaving two identical Dead Banditos, causing all kinds of problems for me (both of me) and changing the future course of events. The astute reader will have already sensed the similarity between this concept and the Editions Concept of the Many Worlds Interpretation of Quantum Mechanics. If there *are* many "editions" of us living in many different worlds simultaneously, maybe these editions are literary editions, as in this case.

you put this book down and forget about it. Go read some
Erma Bombeck.

> *You are not thinking. You are merely being logical.*
> —Niels Bohr to Einstein
> during their great debate on
> Quantum Mechanics

✳ 17 ✳

Busted Banditos

I am beginning to worry about José. It has now been nearly two months since we left Colombia and he seems to be withdrawing further into himself as we move north. He has insisted that I double his studying time to two hours each evening and has begun to ask me unanswerable metaphysical questions. When I fail to answer, he stalks off and sits with High Pockets, cleaning and oiling his Thompson submachine gun until dawn. I can generally hear High Pockets whining on these occasions, so I know José is speaking to him. José *knows* that High Pockets doesn't understand Spanish.

But then the next day he'll jump up and greet the day with his usual Bandito Enthusiasm, forgetting about his brooding sleeplessness. A strange and complicated savage is my eternal friend.

I think I know the cause of José's Bandito Angst: Tina's father. In the last two months we've sent at least three dozen messages, each one from a few miles north of the last. A line connecting them and extending north on its own (our protracted path, as any child could see) *exactly* bisects Sausalito. This precise geometric planning was also José's idea and we went several mountain ranges out of our way to pull it off. And still Tina's father has been silent.

José's obsession with Tina's father finally got us into some serious trouble. He has been insisting we get a copy of each and every *International Trib* in order to check for responses. As you can imagine, this has not been easy. Generally, we find a small town, lurk in the jungle until dark, bolt in, swipe a paper (we've run out of money), then hightail it for the nearest Bandito Stronghold we can locate. We then sit down and peruse the classified section for ads addressed to "Mr. Quark."

This technique worked out fairly well until we crossed the border into southern Mexico last week.

Actually, our capture and subsequent incarceration was mostly High Pockets' fault, but he's been suffering from a slight case of doggy depression since leaving his girlfriend in Costa Rica, so José and I haven't come down too hard on him.

Anyway, we came across this small border town called Motozintla one afternoon. José and I climbed a tree and settled in, waiting for dark, meanwhile keeping an eye on the pueblo for unusual activity. High Pockets isn't too adept at climbing trees, so I told him to stay on the ground and keep a low profile.

I must have nodded out at some point because the next thing I knew José was shaking my arm and whispering excitedly for me to wake up.

He was visibly upset and as soon as I looked in the direction he was pointing I understood why: A platoon of *federales* was chasing High Pockets around the main square of Motozintla.

"Shit," I said. High Pockets was tearing around in circles, his tongue flapping ridiculously along his left flank. I was impressed by his broken-field style of running but eventually he tired and was caught by two *federales* with a blanket. They threw it over him like a net, wrestled him to the ground, handcuffed his front and rear paws, then carted him off to the calaboose.

I looked at José. Seeing High Pockets treated unkindly put him right on the brink of a Bandito Temper Flare-Up. He cocked his Thompson, flung it over his shoulder and clambered down the tree. I heard him jump to the ground, then curse. I looked down and immediately realized why: Another platoon of *federales* had surrounded the tree and had us both dead to rights.

"Shit," I said. At this point the branch I was sitting on broke. I paid a very brief homage to Sir Isaac Newton and his equations pertaining to falling bodies, then struck the ground and lost consciousness.*

When I came to, José was carrying me through town piggyback-style. Most of the residents had turned out to watch the *federales* march us to jail. As we entered, I heard a plane roar overhead, its engines misfiring badly.**

We were escorted into a small, bleak room and told to sit.

José put me down and helped me to one of two chairs set up in the middle of the room. Three heavily armed *federales* tied José and me to the chairs.

---

*I didn't have time to review Einstein's General Theory of Relativity, which also deals with Gravitation.

**Another TTF: I have a confession to make. This last sentence is a Time Travel Sentence (TTS). In other words, I added it at a later date after I found out some things. I did hear a plane but it wouldn't have occurred to me to mention it if there wasn't a payoff somewhere in the future. I have noticed that in most narratives, if you come across a seemingly irrelevant passage (or image in a movie) you can be sure somebody is trying to pull some bullshit on you. A piece of advice: In narratives and in life, pay attention to irrelevancies. They sometimes come back to haunt you.

I heard José curse again. When my eyes regained their ability to focus, I realized what he was pissed about: High Pockets was leashed to a leaky waterpipe, his jaws tied shut by a bandana. He was trying to whine but all that came out was sort of a nasal squeak from his nostrils.

This fat greasy colonel with epaulets and about a kilo of medals hanging from his chest leaned over and grinned at me. He was trying to intimidate me, but succeeded only in making my eyes water from the stench of salsa and tequila on his breath.

I broke the silence by inquiring as to how he had managed to capture us.

My question produced the desired effect: He straightened up and began pacing, thereby getting his fart breath out of my face.

Extrapolating from his explanation, I more or less figured out what had happened. As I mentioned, High Pockets had the doggy blues. He missed his Bandito Bitch from Costa Rica so much that he disobeyed my order to lie low under the tree and instead wandered into town, presumably to find a replacement for his lost love.

He was spotted sniffing behinds by the local constable, who recognized High Pockets from mug shots that had been circulated all over South and Central America. He immediately called the *federales*.

Colonel Stink Bomb then bragged that he had figured if High Pockets was in the area, it was likely José and I were also.

He didn't notice the sarcastic edge to my voice when I complimented him on this brilliant deduction.

He nodded, then rambled on. He explained he had his men fan out in the jungle to find us. They probably never would have succeeded (we were high up and well hidden in the tree) if High Pockets hadn't left one of his patented meat-loaves directly below us.

I looked at High Pockets. He was staring at me apologetically. He knew he'd fucked up.

"Don't worry about it," I said in English.

High Pockets tried to whine in response but, again, hardly anything came out.

Colonel Burrito Breath demanded to know who I was talking to and what I had said.

When I told him I was talking to High Pockets and that I had told him not to worry about it, he whipped out a rubber hose and waved it in front of my face, meanwhile cursing me, Johnny Carson, the devaluation of the peso, his fat, lazy wife and, for some reason, the Pacific Ocean.

At this point, José began to sing "Row, Row, Row Your Boat." Colonel Tarantula Tonsils stopped in midtirade and squinted at him.

I suppressed a grin. I knew what José was doing: He was attempting to conjure up his Bandito Buddy from the O-Zone, figuring that if anyone could get us out of this mess, it would be a Quantum Bandito.

The three *federales* started yelling at José to shut up but he was too busy scouring Alternative Branches of Reality to deal with threats from the Here and Now.

Colonel Trench Mouth had one of his men plug up José's mouth with a banana. It's difficult to carry a tune with a banana stuffed in your mouth, but José was on autopilot and continued. "Row, Row, Row Your Boat" now sounded sort of like "Oh, Oh, Oh Er Oat."

It was obvious that neither José nor High Pockets was in any condition to be interrogated, so Colonel Menendez (he finally introduced himself) turned his full attention on Yours Truly.

He rattled off questions like an AK-47 stuck on full automatic: Who did we come to Mexico to assassinate? How many terrorists did we bring with us? How many Cubans were involved? How do we communicate with the Kremlin? How many nuclear weapons did we have and where were they?

At this point I interrupted Colonel Menendez and told him I would confess everything if he'd shut his trap for a minute.

He grunted in satisfaction, informed one of his men that we weren't as tough as was rumored, then told me to go ahead.

I started at the beginning, with José's mugging of Tina's family. I reviewed the concept of Tina's nymphomania and how it related to all of our Space-Time Coordinates (I made sure to mention that Colonel Menendez himself was now linked forever to Tina, her nymphomania, the concealed diaphragm and her betrayal of Tom and Gary), and how, more than anyone, Tina's father was at the bottom of all this.

I then began one of my crash courses on the Underlying Nature of Reality.*

"*Silencio!*" Colonel Menendez roared at the mention of Schrödinger's Bandito. He ordered his men to take us outside and have us shot.

Ten minutes later I was tied to a stake in the courtyard. High Pockets was leashed to another stake on my right and José to one on my left. He still had the banana sticking out of his mouth and continued his "Row, Row, Row Your Boat" mantra.

Ten or twelve soldiers were lined up in front of us, rifles at the ready. The Captain of the firing squad asked me if I'd like

---

*I did this as much for myself as for Colonel Menendez. I already had the feeling that our situation could easily get out of hand, so I wanted to put our predicament in its proper perspective.

a cigarette. I told him no, I had quit recently, but thanks anyway. He asked if I wanted a blindfold. I said no, give mine to
José. The guy looked at José, then remarked that he didn't
think José needed one since his eyes were closed.

A short argument ensued. We were interrupted by Colonel
Menendez. He was bellowing from inside the jail to hurry up
and get it over with and to make sure the lunatic in the middle
(me) got a few extra rounds on general principle.

I yelled back that he probably wasn't such a big shot in a
few Alternative Branches of Reality.

I then realized the men in the firing squad had cocked their
pieces and were aiming at High Pockets.

"Wait a fucking second!" I yelled in Spanish. "What about
his blindfold!"

Another argument ensued but the Captain finally backed
down and fitted both José and High Pockets with blind-
folds.

"That's better," I mumbled. I looked to my left. José had apparently returned from his travels. He spat out the banana and
asked me why he couldn't see anything. When I told him he
was blindfolded, he said, "Ahh," nodded sagely, then inquired
as to what was going on.

When I told him we were all about to be shot, he got
pissed off.

The timing was perfect. Just as José erupted in a Full-
Blown Bandito Temper Flare-Up, three or four explosions went
off, destroying most of the jail. I caught a glimpse of the Edition of Colonel Menendez that occupied this Branch of Reality fly out the window and fall to the ground like a sack of
doorknobs.

Automatic-weapons fire from the surrounding jungle scattered the firing squad, most of which beat cheeks down the
road without returning fire or looking back.

Meanwhile, José had broken his restraints and untied High Pockets, and he was now freeing me.

José had forgotten to remove High Pockets' blindfold and muzzle, so it took us a few minutes to chase him down and remove the goddamn things. We then bolted through the chaos to what was left of the jail, grabbed our weapons and José's sombrero and escaped into the jungle.

For the last five days, or should I say nights, we've been continuing our trek north, undaunted by the Motozintla fiasco. We now travel only after dark, and it's grueling to say the least. Cutting your way through rain forests at night is tricky business, but both José and I agree we're too hot to show our faces in daylight.

We've been careful to make contact only with Banditos whom José is familiar with or who have been recommended by other Trusted Banditos. The bounty on our heads is now over $500,000, so we always have to be on the lookout for Treacherous Banditos. We have managed to continue our literary barrage to Sausalito via José's Bandito Connections, but we've missed one or two issues of the *Trib* because of the danger involved in getting them. As far as we can tell, Tina's father is still refusing to deal with us, at least directly.

One thing has been bothering José, High Pockets and me. We all have this weird feeling we're being followed. Not tracked in the usual Indian sense; we'd have blown away anybody pulling that shit weeks ago. José, with his Bandito Sixth Sense, was the first to feel it, then High Pockets, then myself. It's almost as if someone has sent out very sensitive feelers, trying to gauge our movements. We don't think it's a government either. Saturation strafing and napalm are more their style. No, some bizarre force, some possibly sinister force, is scrutinizing us for some reason. Waiting. Waiting for what? We have no concrete idea, but both José and I suspect it has something to do with Tina's father.

The concept of entropy dictates that when anything happens, it makes the universe a more disorderly place.

—Michael Talbot

Hello Ramon, Good-bye Ramon

Except for his tendency to severely damage his aircraft and injure passengers, Ramon was considered a decent pilot by rural Mexican standards. And he owned his own business, he quickly pointed out to the three gringos. He owed no one. "Nada, fucking nada." Then he hit them up for a beer.

He had seen these types before. CIA was written all over them. From the license plate of their rental car to the ridiculous clothes the big gringo wore, it was obvious they had just driven up from Mexico City and were ripe for the plucking. The smaller gringo, the one who sounded like he was from Texas, would be the one to talk to about money, since the big gringo was drunk and hostile. The third gringo was an undercover drug agent, Ramon figured. Long red hair, ponytail, always smoking a joint, talking loco. And the dog. Why would these government gringos bring along this crazy dog? No matter, Ramon thought. It was always the same with these stupid *Nortes*. Always looking for something. If they wanted to find a gringo, a

Colombiano and another dog wandering around in the jungle, it would cost them. *Muchos pesos. Muchos.*

As Ramon was thinking these thoughts, Robert shattered his tequila bottle across Ramon's forehead.

Ramon woke up, bound and gagged, in his hangar, his old twin-engine Beechcraft missing. He never saw it again.*

As you sit there and read this book, subatomic particles are passing through your body at the rate of several per minute.

—James S. Trefil

---

*The astute reader is obviously aware that I wrote this chapter in some dim future, after I had found out some things. I also admit I was just taking a wild stab at what Ramon was thinking, but I wanted to try my hand at this Omniscient Observer Attitude. By the way, I may have *written* this chapter in the future, but it isn't a Time Travel Chapter (TTC) in the same sense that I use Time Travel Footnotes. In some sense, we've gone sideways in the space-time continuum, rather than backward or forward.

✳ 19 ✳

Bronx Banditos

José, High Pockets and I are a mere hundred or so miles south of the U.S. border now, and we have run out of Bandito Strongholds to hide out in. As a matter of fact, the last few Banditos we've run into offended José's Bandito Sensibilities. I can see his point, to tell you the truth, although I thought I was above such matters. The last so-called Full-Blown Bandito we ran into was supposedly a distant cousin of José's, but José claims that this couldn't possibly be true. The guy wore J.C. Penney shoes and spent most of his time listening to Herb Alpert tapes on his Sony Walkman instead of taking care of Bandito Affairs. I had told José that he should expect this kind of thing as we move north into civilization, but he was so agitated by this Phony Bandito that we camped out in the jungle that night.

We didn't even bother bringing up the New Physics or Cosmology with these, the sleaziest, sorriest-looking Banditos I've ever seen. They looked like a gang of Puerto Ricans from the South Bronx, as a matter of fact.

By the way: Yesterday they showed themselves. Whoever's tracking us, that is. They were in an old twin-engine Beechcraft and they appeared suddenly from the south, whence we'd come. The plane was at treetop level and flying very erratically. José, High Pockets and I hit the dirt, José tackling and covering Pepe. They passed about fifteen feet over our heads, showering us with propeller-shredded vegetation, then kept going.

The sound of the old plane's engines faded, then increased slowly in volume. They were coming back. José was ready this time. As they passed over our heads again, he opened up with his Thompson. I saw a line of thumbnail-size holes stitch the undercarriage. This time they didn't come back, but they're still out there somewhere. José now thinks they're bounty hunters, but I'm sticking to my original intuition that they somehow have something to do with Tina's father.

Something happened a couple weeks ago that came as a great psychological relief to José, even though I had told him it would happen all along. Here it is: Tina's father got in touch. This is the ad we found in the *International Herald Tribune*:

"MR. QUARK: IT APPEARS THAT WE HAVE MUCH IN COMMON."

Since this first message he has hardly been able to keep his trap shut. Last week:

"MR. QUARK: OUR GUEST ROOM IS WAITING."

And so forth.

José is asleep now, as are High Pockets and Pepe, our little burro. The campfire is dying, the sky is clear and crisp, but I am unable to sleep, although I am still essentially at peace with myself.

Perhaps it is our forthcoming showdown with Tina's father

that has me on edge. I know it is on José's mind. He is afraid Tina's father will be angry at him for the mugging incident.

I assured José that as soon as Tina's father is made aware of all the facts, the mugging will be seen as a necessary—no, *inevitable*—occurrence in a chain of coincidences that lead to all of our individual Space-Time Coordinates and Worldviews.

I have had, however, occasional doubts about my attitude toward Tina's father, and wonder if my relationship with him is a little strange. Why is it so important that I confront him? Why do I consider him my spiritual father? Why must I have his approval?

Of course, Tina's father will demand an explanation for the hundreds of cryptic messages I sent (or had sent from various Bandito Strongholds).*

I assume from his recent missives in the *Trib* that Tina's father will be all ears. I hope he's ready. I hope I'm ready. I hope José is ready. I hope Gary, Tom and Tina are ready. This is an awesome responsibility I have taken on.

There is no force of gravity as such. Rather, a celestial body merely pays attention to what it finds in its neighborhood.

—Albert Einstein

---

*The reader should keep in mind that there is no reason why Tina's father should connect me and my messages with the mugging or anything else. I'm relieved that he no longer doubts my existence, but his perception of me is still a missing piece in this weird jigsaw puzzle I am assembling.

20

The High and the Mighty

Jim taped a felt map of South and Central America to the bulkhead just aft of the copilot's seat. Embedded in the map were dozens of pins with little dated labels. The pins showed an unmistakable pattern: They started in the Sierra Nevadas Mountains in Colombia, then crept slowly north through Panama, Costa Rica, Nicaragua and on to Mexico. The last pin was dated just a few days before.

Jim squinted at the map, then drew a pencil line along a projected path. "They'll probably follow this here ridge. José likes to keep to high ground."

Robert had a healthy belt of mescal. "Flash boy, fire this sucker up, buddy." He belched, then farted painfully. His diet of tequila, tortillas and salsa had given him a serious case of "ring of fire."

Flash squinted through the marijuana smoke at the unfamiliar instrument panel. His right arm was in a cast and sticking upward at a forty-five-degree angle, like a Nazi salute, so he reached over with his left hand and tried a different combination of up/down switch positions, then hit the start button again.

Nothing happened. He had never flown a Beech-18 before and was unsure of its starting sequence. All the switch labels had worn off long ago, but Flash was used to that sort of thing. Using his semirandom method of evaluating a switch's function, he tried another combination. The left engine turned over and fired up.

"Okay, Aileron." He pointed out a red-tipped overhead toggle switch. "That's the left-side magneto."

Aileron, sitting in the copilot's seat, whined.

"This must be the right-side magneto." Flash was imprinting the switch system into his short-term memory bank. The 60's had short-circuited his long-term memory functions, but since he had no recollection of what long-term memory was, he never noticed its absence.

The right engine fired up. Flash gave Jim and Robert the "thumbs up." Jim displaced Aileron in the copilot's seat and yelled over the roaring engines, "How much fuel we got?"

"Fuck if I know!" Flash yelled back. "Don't worry about it!"

"We gotta find those two maniacs before they get in trouble again!"

Flash nodded vigorously. "Treetop level!" He gave both engines full throttle.

An hour later they were barreling along the ridge that Jim had calculated José would favor for the trek north. Flash was trimming the topmost layer of the rain forest, using the big twin props like a giant lawnmower. Occasional branches and chunks of debris flew in the open side-cockpit windows.

Robert passed the mescal up to Flash. Flash passed the joint back to Robert. Jim nursed a fifth of Cuervo Gold.

Both props were slightly bent from plowing through trees, and the old airframe was vibrating badly. It was in precisely this fashion that Flash had demolished the "Loaded Star" a few weeks ago. As usual, he and Aileron walked away from the crash, Flash with a broken arm, Aileron with his tail badly bent.*

"You see that?" Jim was trying to look back through the window on his side. "I saw something. I think it was them."

"Gimme the bottle," Robert said, groping for the mescal. He pulled a grenade from his plaid jacket and slurred, "Turn around. I'll drop this on 'em as a sig-signal." He belched horribly, filling the cockpit with tequila-and-salsa nerve gas.

"Jesus fucking *Christ!*" Jim bellowed. He and Flash stuck their heads out the side windows to avoid suffocation. Aileron bounded aft in fright.

Flash made a sweeping U-turn and began to retrace the swath he had cut through the jungle.

The cockpit had just recovered from Robert's gastric assault when José's volley of .45 slugs sliced through the aircraft from nose to tail.

Nobody was hit, but the boys voted to *change tactics.* They decided that their rescue mission would have to be *toned down.*

---

*I told you all that there would be a payoff to the seemingly irrelevant statement I made back in Chapter 17, as José and I were being taken to jail. I quote: "As we entered, I heard a plane roar overhead, its engines misfiring badly." Then, if you recall, I subjected you to a Time Travel Footnote (TTF) and admitted that I had added this sentence at a later date, after I had found out some things. The astute reader has already figured out that what I discovered was that it had been Flash, Aileron, Robert and Jim in that plane. They had been following us and spotted our capture. After they landed in a nearby pasture, Robert blew up the jail (his second so far) while Jim and Flash opened up on the firing squad, effecting our escape from certain death. Flash and Aileron then took off to try to relocate us but unfortunately crashed soon after take off.

The very astute reader is obviously aware that this footnote is itself a TTF, albeit of a different sort from the other (I hesitate to use the word "past") TTFs. This is a TTF in a TTC (Time Travel Chapter), which makes it sort of a TTF to the second power (TTF²).

They would take a *different tack*. All sorts of euphemisms were thrown around, but the truth of the matter was that José and his big-bore submachine gun made everybody nervous, even Robert. Until they were able to identify themselves as "friend-lies," they would keep out of sight altogether. They would have to rely on Plan B, which had already been launched anyway.*

There is no time which flows equally for all observers. "Now," "sooner," "later," and "simultaneous" are relative to the frame of reference of the observer.   —Albert Einstein

---

*The astute reader will have noticed that the second to last paragraph of this chapter coincides temporally with a section of the previous chapter that dealt with my perception of José's anti-aircraft activities on the ground. This is the same event viewed from two different reference points. Let me quote from both chapters:

I saw a line of thumbnail-size holes stitch the undercarriage. (Chapter 19)

This is what I actually saw, as relayed to you in the previous chapter. Now, in this current chapter, I cop my Omniscient Observer Attitude (for the last time) and take us where I have never been:

The cockpit had just recovered from Robert's gastric assault when José's volley of .45 slugs sliced through the aircraft from nose to tail. (Chapter 20)

This is one event as perceived from two different points of reference simultaneously by the same person. Not easy to pull off, even in a simple narrative.

I do not intend to try the reader's patience here with another comparison to the Many Worlds Interpretation of Quantum Mechanics or its "Editions" concept. This would be redundant, not to mention repetitious. The reader is free to make any associations he or she wishes to make, however.

21

Blind Banditos

A lot has happened. . . . Wait a minute—I like that. *A lot has happened.* A very Subatomic concept. No matter how fast you repeat "a lot has happened," you still haven't said it fast enough to invalidate the statement.*

Of course, certain scientists with Cosmological Leanings might take issue with this. They may say, for example, that no matter how long you *wait* between repetitions of "a lot has happened," hardly anything has happened at all. In the grand scheme, hardly anything *ever* happens. Those two concepts—"a lot has happened" and "hardly anything has happened"—may seem to reflect a serious difference in outlooks. But this is not necessarily the case. What you see is as much a function of where you stand as what you're looking at.

Cosmologists seem to keep backing up to get a wider view of things while we Subatomic Enthusiasts have trouble with

---

*I am, of course, referring to how much stuff happens between repetitions.

crossed eyes and smudged noses from trying to get a closer look at Underlying Reality.

If a Cosmologist agreed to a meeting of the minds with a Subatomic Kind of Guy like me, we'd probably meet somewhere in the middle, in the Twilight Zone of our two Worldviews. That Twilight Zone (to us) would be the World as You All Know It. The world of Bananas, Banditos, Contrabandistas and Dope Lords.

Anyway, about a week ago José, High Pockets and I were squatting in a huge drainpipe just outside Tijuana with a couple dozen wetbacks, also America-bound. We had a few hours to kill before the sprint across the border, so José thought he'd give the poor peasants a quick lecture in order to put their miserable existences in the proper perspective.

Since we were all fellow travelers, José thought he'd delve into the concept of travel. He first explained that reality is a Space-Time Continuum and bolting across the U.S. border is an example of travel in space. Why not, since space and time are aspects of the same something, consider the possibility of travel in time?

Seeing José standing in the mouth of a drainpipe, holding a pint bottle of mescal and a Thompson submachine gun and rambling on about Time Travel, made some of the wetbacks nervous. A few tried to inch their way out without being noticed, but High Pockets was sitting by José's side and discouraged this type of behavior with bared fangs and a low, menacing growl.

José had a belt of mescal, then got down to the nitty-gritty. Motion in time only proceeds in one direction in the Macrocosmic World, he explained, from the past to present, then on to the future.

A pregnant pause punctuated by a belch.

This is an illusory effect, he explained, then delved insightfully into Einstein's Special Theory of Relativity. Nothing in the Universe is absolute, he asserted, except for the speed of light. Moreover, as an entity approaches that speed (relative to its coordinate system), several bizarre things begin to manifest themselves, such as time dilation.

At this point it started to rain. We were all protected from the downpour except José, who paced in front of the drainpipe, gesturing with his mescal bottle. The wetbacks stared wide-eyed at him as he reviewed Einstein's work.

One of the best proofs we have of time dilation, José continued, is the behavior of muons, which are formed when certain cosmic rays bombard our upper atmosphere. They are very fast Subatomic Particles. Some travel at .99 percent of the speed of light. They are also very short-lived, so short-lived that none should be expected to reach the surface of the earth before decaying into other Subatomic Particles. In fact many do.

José finished off his mescal and tossed the bottle over his shoulder. By now it was raining like a son of a bitch and water was cascading off his sombrero in sheets. He had to raise his voice. To us as observers, José yelled, muons "live" seven times longer than they would at rest, a result of time dilation. This, he added, is true to a lesser or greater extent of all Subatomic Entities, of all Cosmic Banditos.

There was a violent crack of thunder.

The downpour increased further in intensity.

José was lit up in chiaroscuro by a bolt of lightning.

The above special effects made the wetbacks even more nervous. Several crossed themselves, some mumbling about "el Diablo" and pointing at José.

José finally got to the point, wetback-wise. Why bother to traverse a heavily protected border, he postulated, when just a few years ago, say a hundred, it was totally unprotected? If we could find an incredibly powerful gravitational field like a black hole, José roared over the din, we could distort the fabric of Space-Time and find ourselves a mellower Coordinate System, saunter across the border and catch a stagecoach to Sausalito, then zip back to this Coordinate System so you guys could pick bananas* or whatever and the rest of us could get on with this crucial matter of Tina's father!

It was a mouthful, I admit, but José was on a roll. He immediately digressed all the way back to the beginning, to his mugging of Tina's family.** He was just beginning to review the concept of Tina's nymphomania when I heard a roaring sound coming up the drainpipe. Evidently someone had opened a floodgate. As I turned to look, I was struck by flowing debris and lost consciousness.

When I came to it was daylight and I was somewhat disoriented. My first impression was that I was in the back of a limousine watching the "Today" show and holding a glass of champagne.

I shut my eyes† and massaged my temples. I heard a giggle. Shit, I thought to myself, then opened my right eye. Not only was I still in the back of the limo but now a bikini-clad teenage girl was sitting next to me, also holding a glass of champagne.

"Tina, is that you?" I muttered, thinking I had actualized in some weird Alternative Branch of reality where Tina's path and mine had crossed in a normal manner. Perhaps we had just gotten married or were on our way to the prom. But why would

---

*José had never been to Sausalito and was unaware of the fact that bananas don't grow there.

**A TTF: Looking back from the future it appears to me that the mugging of Tina's family had taken on a Big Bangesque quality. "In the beginning there was the mugging of Tina's Family"—that kind of thing.

†Over the years, I have found I can get rid of most hallucinations by closing my eyes.

Tina be wearing a bikini? Limousines would seem to call for more formal attire. On the other hand . . .

"My name isn't Tina. It's Marcy," the girl said, then giggled again.

"Oh," I replied. I paused contemplatively. "Listen, uh, Marcy, could you fill me in on a few things, like where we are and where we're going? I had a rough night last night."

"Sure, we're like going to Newport to like hang out."

"Hang out," I repeated. I was still feeling woozy, so I had a swallow of champagne to clear my head.

"Your friend is like really gnarly," Marcy said, then giggled again.

"My friend?"

"Yeah, like the dude with the awesome hat."

I looked toward the front. The limo driver was wearing a sombrero.

Sitting next to him was a strange-looking dog with his tongue hanging out.

"José?" I ventured. I was wondering whether I was still the Edition of myself that was last heard from sitting in a drainpipe in Mexico with a bunch of wetbacks listening to José give a lecture on Quantum Theory and Time Travel.

The driver turned around and grinned. It was José, all right.

"*Cómo estás, hermano?*" he inquired.

"*No sé,*" I replied.

High Pockets barked, then erupted in a sneezing attack.

I breathed a sigh of relief and sat back.

I still haven't found out how we got across the border or where the limo and Marcy came from, but I do know that we spent a pleasant couple of days in Newport Beach, California.

Although we were still flat broke, thanks to José we were well taken care of. He had had the insight to fill his sombrero full of Mexican sensimilla buds before we crossed the border. We spent most of the first night in a hot tub smoking joints with the locals and most of the next day lurking on the beach.

José was quite popular with the kids. He even got a standing ovation for his go-for-it style of Bandito Body Surfing. He hit the water wearing his Fruit of the Loom shorts, crisscrossed bandoliers and sombrero, then proceeded to wow the local surf crew by continually riding ten-foot swells right into the jetty at a surf spot called the Wedge.

High Pockets, on the other hand, had problems. He doesn't care for poodles (neither do I) and the area was lousy with them. About a half dozen of the little bastards ganged up on him while he was snoozing on the beach. If the reader has gotten the idea that High Pockets is somewhat on the timid side, let me set the record straight right here.

High Pockets may be intimidated by jaguars, Rowdy Banditos, old Indians who belch violently, crazed *federales* and artillery fire, but he doesn't take any shit from other dogs, especially dogs with little ribbons in their little hairdos.

The dogfight was short and one-sided. Suffice to say the doggy beauty salons of Newport Beach (not to mention the veterinarians) were very busy that day.*

I made discreet inquiries about Tina, figuring she might have cut a sexual swath through Newport on her way back to Sausalito, but to tell you the truth, I had trouble understanding the brand of English spoken around there.

For example, I have no way of knowing whether Tina is tubular or nontubular since I have no idea what the concept of tubularity means.**

---

*As I have mentioned, José and I love dogs, but we are of the opinion that poodles are actually some sort of rodent.

**I unsuccessfully attempted to find out whether the concept of tubularity is related to the concept of singularity, which occurs near the center of a Black

Anyway, José, High Pockets and I have spent the last few days on the road and have reached San Francisco, gateway to Sausalito.

Being financially destitute, we've been ensconced in a downtown mission for alcoholics and atheists. In order to get something to eat, we are forced to listen to some cretin lecture on God and what He has in mind for us.

They refuse to feed High Pockets, even though he sits through the lectures like everyone else. I had words with the morons who run the place about this. These people have the attitude that since High Pockets is a dog, he has no soul and therefore is not deserving of sustenance.

Luckily, José was explaining Quantum Theory to Hispanic hobo and didn't overhear this so-called missionary's view of High Pockets.* José would've shot the guy on the spot.** José and High Pockets are thick as thieves in spite of the language barrier. (As I have mentioned, High Pockets doesn't understand Spanish.)

High Pockets is hip to a fact I learned the hard way over the years: If you can only have one friend and ally in your life, choose a Bandito.

Unfortunately, True Banditos are getting more and more difficult to find, what with the encroachment of civilization into the wilds and all. The True Bandito loathes so-called "progress" and the grimy glut of the cities. As he will tell you, a city is good for one thing only: mating. He'll come into a city

---

Hole. It is here that infinitely strong gravitational forces compress matter to zero volume, thereby destroying the very fabric of Space-Time.
*Even though José doesn't understand English, I'm sure he would've gotten the drift from my yelling and gesticulating and High Pockets' stomach rumblings.
**José had to leave his Thompson submachine gun in Mexico, but he kept his .45 automatic and I my 9mm. Our little burro, Pepe, found a good home on a farm just outside Tijuana.

once or twice a year, stalk around like the magnificent predator that he is, mate as often as possible, then retreat to his natural habitat, the jungle, usually leaving an impressive array of breathless females in his wake.

Of course, the profound nature of the mission we are on here precludes this kind of behavior. José and I agree that we are too close to Tina's father to think on a carnal level.

We sent our last messages to the whole group (let us not forget Tina, Tom and Gary) two days ago and have been waiting for a reply (in the *San Francisco Chronicle*) before we move in for the Subatomic Kill, so to speak. This morning we got our answer. Here it is:

> "MR. QUARK: DINNER.
> TOMORROW AT 8.
> INFORMAL."

In order to get everything done that had to get done we needed money, so High Pockets and I went down to Fisherman's Wharf. I sat down in the dirt with a tin cup, sunglasses and High Pockets (as my seeing eye dog) and begged up about $20. José took off on his own and, God bless him, met me back at the mission with nearly $200. He wouldn't tell me how he got it, but from the way he took apart and cleaned his .45, I have my suspicions.

After a lengthy discussion, José and I finally agreed to look up Gary, since he lives in San Francisco. The future seemed very uncertain and we figured this might be our only chance to pay our respects. Unfortunately, our visit to Gary didn't go exactly as planned.

Gary's address is in an area called Noe Valley. We got lost once (José's fault) and got ejected from another bus (High Pockets' fault) before finding Gary's house. After a two-hour stakeout, Gary emerged (I *knew* it was him), walked down his steep street and caught a bus. High Pockets, José and I followed surreptitiously.

He got off rather suddenly, causing the three of us way in the back to scramble madly for the door before it closed. We just made it.

I took one look at the neighborhood and started to get edgy. Gary sauntered over and asked me for a light. I looked at him closely while pretending to grope for a match. He was about twenty or twenty-one, with short blond hair and a slight frame. He wore tight designer jeans, a mauve T-shirt, black cowboy boots and matching leather wristbands. You guessed it. Gary was a flaming homosexual.

This was not a good omen. I made a mental note to ask him about Tina and whether her duplicity had driven him to homosexuality. It was vital that I find out if I was responsible for Gary's drastic change in lifestyle. Had my messages from South America caused him to run sexually amok? There was so much I needed to know.

Gary glanced at José, then at me. He smiled. "You guys new in town?"

"Yeah," I said, then translated the question for José.

"*Sí, sí,*" José said.

"Come on. I'll introduce you around."

He led us up the street, which was teeming with homosexuals. José, with his wonderfully childlike Worldview, didn't notice anything was amiss until Gary led us into this leather bar called the Crisco Disco West.

José was an immediate smash-hit sensation. He was, of course, still dressed in his rawhide-and-buckskin Bandito Outfit, complete with sombrero and bandoliers stuffed with .45 slugs.

"Fabulous!"

"Divine!"

"I'm going to faint!"

"Macho to the max!"

And so forth.

At first José didn't understand any of this. He just smiled and nodded. Almost everybody in the place was wearing studded black leather and chains, so José was being careful. Gary bought us beers. José thanked him, then asked me if everyone in San Francisco was as tough as these guys.

"He's Hispanic!"

"Did you hear him *talk?!*"

"Such an animal!"

And so forth.

High Pockets erupted in a sneezing attack, probably brought on by the overpowering smell of perfume and leather.

I was getting very edgy. I wanted to discuss some vital topics with Gary, but I knew that as soon as José realized what was going on, there was going to be some serious trouble. Major-league trouble.

I didn't have to wait long. This one homosexual asked José for a light, making another homosexual jealous, which made *that* homosexual's boyfriend upset, which set off a Homosexual Chain Reaction that made everyone in the place upset.

At this point, Gary laid his head on José's massive chest and whispered, "Take me home."

High Pockets and I saw it coming and dove for cover.

"Maricón!" José bellowed, but it sounded more like a defective foghorn than a word.

He then pulled his pistol and proceeded to shoot up the Crisco Disco West.

I counted his shots. I knew he always kept one in the chamber, so I waited until nine. I heard José cursing and trying to reload from his bandolier. High Pockets and I jumped up and surveyed the damage. José hadn't shot anyone yet. I knew he was just blowing off steam, but I doubted that the police would be very understanding.

I grabbed him and attempted to drag him outside, pleading with him to be reasonable since we had important work to do. Mentioning Tina's father did the trick. We bolted for a waiting bus across the street. Screaming homosexuals were every-where, giving the scene a surreal, almost Subatomic look.*

José seemed to be limping, so I checked his legs for injuries as we boarded the bus. Gary was wrapped around José's right leg, clutching it in a death grip and whimpering that he would kill himself if José left him.

José reached for his .45 with the obvious intention of put-ting the poor wimp out of his misery, but I got Gary in a hammer-lock, peeled him off José's leg and flung him off the bus.

"No dogs," the driver said, referring to High Pockets. He reopened the doors. Gary was back on his feet and staggering in our direction. Sirens were wailing, homosexuals screaming.

"He's a seeing-eye dog," I said to the driver. This concept had worked earlier in the day when I needed money. The driver was a jovial-looking black guy wearing a beret. His eyes nar-rowed in suspicion.

"You not blind."

"My friend is blind," I said, jerking my head toward José.

"No, he in't. He Mesican."

Gary boarded the bus, his eyes wild with passion. I gave him a swift kick in the stomach, saving his life (José had drawn his piece) and sending him flying back outside into the grow-ing Homosexual Riot.

---

*If you excite either a Subatomic Particle *or* a homosexual, its movement be-comes more frenetic and more random.

I pulled my 9mm and put it to the bus driver's head. "I'm afraid I'm going to have to commandeer this vehicle."

"Okay."

"Get going."

"Where to?"

"Sausalito."

Einstein's Unified Field Theory was an attempt to unite the macrocosmic realm with that of the subatomic. . . . This was the culmination of Einstein's lifelong need to find order in a seemingly disorderly and chaotic universe. . . . Most physicists agree that his attempt failed abysmally.
—Gary Zukav

✳ 22 ✳

Sausalito Banditos

PART I

It has now been over two months since José and I had our showdown with Tina's father, but until now I've been too shaken up to put anything down on paper. José, God bless him, has nursed me back to mental health and I'm starting to feel like I can confront the truth and all the implications of what happened.

I read this manuscript to José not long ago, and we both feel that it is vital that I complete it. Looking at it now, with a little distance between myself and the events depicted, with a little psychological perspective, I see it's obvious that this story is a veritable road map for Lost Souls. But more about that later. First, let me describe our experiences in Sausalito and Berkeley, starting where I left off, with the hijacking of the bus.

We stopped briefly while José herded the other passengers out, meanwhile repelling crazed homosexuals who were trying to board. We managed to escape from the riot just as the police arrived. I had the driver do some evasive maneuvering to shake off possible tails. I still had the weird sensation that we were under the scrutiny, if not the control, of that same force that had manifested itself as an old twin Beechcraft airplane in Mexico. And that that force was somehow linked (possibly in a Subatomic fashion) to Tina's father.

José and High Pockets, innocents that they were, had their heads sticking out one window, enjoying the fresh air and the sight of the Golden Gate Bridge rushing toward us, the sun setting over the Pacific in the background. High Pockets' tongue had unraveled to its full, almost unbelievable length, and was flapping in the breeze, occasionally snapping like a lion tamer's whip. José had one arm around High Pockets' neck and was smiling contentedly. They looked like kids on their way to summer camp instead of a couple desperados careening toward the Unknown.

"Wha' exit?" the driver asked.

"Sausalito," I said.

"They two Sausalito exit."

"Shit."

"Give yo'self up. It go 'lot easy on ya."

I laughed. "We'd all be shot on sight."

"What'd ya do, fer chrissakes?"

"You name it, we did it. We're desperate men."

"Why ya goin' Sausalito?"

"It's a long story."

"Wha' exit? Here come de first." He laughed. "Wee-oow. Dere go de first."

"Get off at the second."

"Okay. By de way, my name Rafer."

"Hi, Rafer."

"Wee-oow. Here we go."

Rafer exited the freeway and, on my orders, drove randomly around suburban Sausalito while José and I shared a fifth of tequila in the back and planned our next move.

We had nearly twenty-four hours to kill before our dinner date with Tina's father (and, presumably, the whole family) and since I had never been in the Bay Area before, I asked Rafer if he had any suggestions as to what a couple of fun-loving guys might do in the way of entertainment.

"I hungry," Rafer said in the way of an answer. It turned out that everyone was hungry, so Rafer pulled the bus into a family-type Italian restaurant just outside town. He parked the bus behind the building out of sight of the road.

"Jus' in case," he said, adjusting his beret.

"In case of what?" I asked.

"Case de po-lice come by, dey don' see de bus." Rafer helped himself to a slug of José's tequila. "Ya'll done stoled munici-pal propitty and done kidnapped a city 'ployee."

"That's right," I said. I had forgotten. It should have occurred to me that I was beginning to lose touch with reality, but Rafer wasn't setting a great example. He had mentally included himself in our organization and was behaving as if we'd been partners in crime for years.

"Ya look like ya needin' some rest," he said to me as we sat down to dinner. "I do de thinkin' fo' a while."

"Okay," I said.

Sausalito Banditos
PART II

After dinner Rafer and José doctored the plates and identification numbers on the bus so we'd have cool wheels for the night. We picked up a case of Cuervo Gold, rolled up some Guajiran buds and hit the road.

Over dinner I had filled Rafer in on our situation with re-spect to the law, Subatomic Phenomena and Tina's father. Rafer wanted in.

José and I discussed it (in Spanish) and agreed, seeing as how Rafer was familiar with the area and had wheels. His level of enthusiasm was acceptable and he liked dogs. On the minus side, he seemed unable to grasp even the most rudimentary as-pects of the New Physics. But the night was young and Rafer soon came up with a concept that immediately appealed to José and me.

I dimly recall Rafer's plan of attack. We would first smoke joints and guzzle tequila. Then we'd find Tina's family's house and make a few passes at it in the bus. The last phase of Rafer's plan was the masterstroke. We would look up Tom and some-how persuade him to join us for a night of dissipation and chaos. Naturally, we would fail to mention who we were until the time was ripe. In the meantime, Tom could fill in many pieces of the Big Puzzle without even knowing it.

It sounded foolproof, but unfortunately things didn't go ex-actly as planned.

The marijuana smoking and tequila swilling went off pretty much without a hitch; then we attempted to locate Tina's fam-ily's house, with Rafer behind the wheel. His hand-eye coordi-nation and motor skills in general were seriously impaired. He kept thinking he was driving his '64 Impala instead of a sixty-foot municipal bus, which has drastically different handling characteristics.

Rafer had claimed to know Sausalito quite well, but it be-came evident that his memory had failed at one crucial inter-section or another when I realized that we were on the Golden Gate Bridge, heading back to San Francisco. When I pointed this out, Rafer said, "Wee-oow," made a crowd-pleasing U-turn and whipped us back to Sausalito.

Sausalito Banditos
PART III

We decided to scrub the strafing mission on Tina's family's house, and zero in on Tom. I gave Rafer the address.

He squinted at it and adjusted his beret. "Mo' 'killya."

This was Rafer's way of requesting more tequila. José handed him the bottle. "Wee-oow," Rafer said after a healthy pull. This expression ("Wee-oow") was apparently very flexible, and equivalent to one of José's "Aahhh," which also could mean just about anything.

Anyway, ten minutes later we were parked in front of an apartment complex overlooking Sausalito Bay. Rafer blared the horn a half dozen times. Lights were turned on up and down the quiet, middle-class street.

"Jesus, don't do that," I said. "We gotta use some subtlety here."

"Mo' 'killya," Rafer said.

"You're holdin' it," I said.

"Wee-oow," Rafer said.

"How're we gonna get Tom out of there?" I asked no one in particular.

"We jus' go on up and invite de dude out," Rafer reasoned. "He sayin' no, we beatin' 'im up, steal de stereo."

I translated the plan to José. He nodded in agreement. "Sí, sí."

The apartment numbering system was completely random. (The place should've been called the Subatomic Arms.) It took about twenty minutes to find Tom's place.

"Wait a minute," I said. I had caught a glimpse of us in the reflection in Tom's curtained front windows. A quick group portrait, so to speak.

I had everybody stand back for a good look: Rafer, with his bus driver's uniform, beret and bottle of tequila, was on our right. Next came High Pockets, his fluorescent tongue hanging to the ground. Then me. I was looking a little weird; something about the eyes, I thought.* José was on the left end of the group, looking like . . . well, like the Full-Blown Bandito that he was. I wondered what Tom would think when he opened the door and saw us standing on his stoop. There was only one way to find out, so I pounded on the door and stepped back into my position in the aforementioned group portrait.

Sausalito Banditos
PART IV

Nobody was home. For some reason I was unprepared for this scenario.

Rafer, God bless him, took command immediately. He picked Tom's front door lock in about four seconds. We ducked inside and locked up.

I was impressed with Tom's apartment. Furnished with mostly natural wood stuff (all sturdy and no-nonsense), it also boasted a reasonable number of healthy plants. The pictures and artwork also indicated that Tom had a normal masculine Worldview. I had worried that I might've caused some horrible psychological miscarriage in Tom, as I had in Gary,

---

*The truth of the matter is this: I had begun to *see* Subatomic Particles. They would dart through the Space-Time Continuum leaving little purple trails. The ones that passed through my body invariably made me tingle and giggle and squirm. I've never mentioned this to anyone before, not even José.

but his apartment indicated that he had weathered my literary bombardment from South and Central America relatively unscathed.

"Wee-oow," Rafer kept repeating as he inventoried Tom's belongings. "Good thing we gots de bus. We take ever'thing but de shitter." He had a pull of tequila. "I find some fools, mebbe we get dat, too."

José and High Pockets were pillaging the refrigerator. "*Quieres comer?*" José inquired. I told him no, I wasn't hungry. He tossed me his bottle of tequila, so I sat down and tried to relax. I turned on the TV with a remote control and attempted to gather my thoughts. José and High Pockets joined me on the couch and proceeded to stuff their faces with leftovers and improvised sandwiches.

"Ahhh," José said.

"Wee-oow," Rafer agreed from the bedroom.

At this point the front door swung open and Tom breezed in, carrying a bag of groceries. He was halfway to the kitchen before he noticed he had problems. He looked at the couch and saw a Bandito pointing a .45 automatic at him, a strange-looking dog with his teeth bared and a slice of bologna hanging from his lower jowl and me with my 9mm and Subatomic Scowl. He looked toward the kitchen and saw a psychotic municipal bus driver holding a meat cleaver.

I could tell by the look on Tom's face that we could forget about a night on the town with the guys. He looked at each of us again, then settled on me.

"It's you, isn't it?" he stammered. "The lunatic from South America."

"Yes," I said.

"Oh, God."

"Sit down."

"Yes, sir." Tom put the groceries down and sat stiffly on a dining room chair. José, Rafer, High Pockets and I joined him at the table.

"Mebbe we tie 'im up," Rafer suggested.

"Not yet," I said. I was regaining control over my faculties.

"Tom," I said softly, "we have some things to go over, wouldn't you say?"

Tom was confused. "Uh, I . . . I don't know."

José cocked his .45 and put it to Tom's head.

"Where do we start?" Tom said quickly.

"Let's start with Tina, okay?"

Sausalito Banditos
PART V

Tom cracked after four hours of intensive interrogation. He had sweated through his shirt and business suit and was trembling violently. José helped him into the bedroom so he could lie down for a while. He immediately slipped into a deep existential coma, however, and was unavailable for questioning for the remainder of the night.

My fears proved to be well-founded. I had shaken up Tom in a fundamental psychological way, as well as Gary. Tom had taken my original note (explaining Tina's treachery) in relative stride, and was only mildly curious about the origin of the missive.

Tom claimed that the hundreds of other messages I had sent were thrown away unopened, but I think he is repressing painful memories. I think he read every note, possibly memorized them, then denied them when their cumulative impact

showed Tom the utter uselessness of his life. When he was con-
fronted by the harsh reality of me and my gang, it all came
back to him in one nightmarish rush—hence the coma.

Tom was an insurance salesman in his early thirties, and he
fancied himself quite the man-about-town. He drove a vintage
Porsche and played racquetball. He belonged to the local
country club and was a competent tennis player. He shot a
round of golf in the low 80s.

He had met Tina at a country club function and banged her
that night in a sand trap on the 12th hole. The next day she
had left for her Caribbean vacation with her parents. Tom
never saw her again and hardly remembered her at all. When I
translated this admission to José he let out one of his "Ahhhs."
I knew exactly what he meant. This is what this particular
"Ahhh" signified: Tom was an unwitting clown in our Subatomic Circus. By all rational logic, he didn't deserve to be in
the bizarre situation he found himself in. Tina had been a casual affair on the 12th hole fairway bunker, nothing more. For
this flippant tryst, however, Tom paid dearly. He had been
forced to cough up his Worldview.

If he ever came out of his coma, his old perception of reality would have to be scrapped. It was woefully obsolete.

José and I were in Tom's bedroom discussing the implications of all this, José mopping Tom's feverish brow, when we
heard Rafer yell, "Wee-oow!" from the living room. We
checked our weapons and beat cheeks out there, ready for
trouble.

It was the TV that caused Rafer's outburst. Even José was
taken aback. The broadcast showed a SWAT team surrounding Rafer's municipal bus outside Tom's apartment. It was a
live report via a shaky, handheld minicam. I peeked out
Tom's front window. Yep, they were out there in real life,
too.

The reporter was explaining the facts of the hijacking, and flashed a head-and-shoulders shot of Rafer.

"Wee-oow," Rafer said. Everyone on the tube was concerned about Rafer's safety.

They flashed mug shots of José, High Pockets and me, the voice-over accusing us of being bloodthirsty terrorists.

"Ahh," José said again.

Several federal agents were interviewed. Each had a different theory as to why we had hijacked the bus. None even came close to the Subatomic Truth.

Sausalito Banditos

PART VI

We were forced to keep a low profile that night. Eventually the Feds had Rafer's bus towed to the FBI Crime Lab in San Francisco, presumably to be analyzed for clues or evidence or whatnot.*

I have to give the Feds credit. They were learning. All we had left in the bus was a half case of tequila and an empty box of Milk Bone Flavor Snacks for Large Dogs. They had figured out who we were by these meager clues. Possibly they had interviewed a few homosexuals from the Crisco Disco West. Maybe they interviewed Gary. Who knows? That would be an interesting concept. He never found out that we were responsible, José and I, for his fall to faggotry. God only knows what kind of breakdown he'd have if he did find out. His unrequited love

---

*Once again the TV news had come in handy for discovering the repercussions of our behavior.

for José would certainly complicate an already complex situation.

Anyway, José, Rafer, High Pockets and I had a sitdown at about noon the next day. José was tired, having stayed up all night attending to Tom, who was still comatose.

We cracked a fresh bottle of tequila and began planning our next move. As far as we could tell, the Feds had cleared out early in the morning after questioning a few neighbors.

We had about eight hours until our dinner date with Tina's father and everyone wanted to do something constructive. Rafer wanted to knock over a bank or armored car. José wanted to review Quantum Theory with me in case the subject came up at dinner. I needed some fresh air to clear my head and regroup my thoughts. We settled on a compromise. This was it: We would steal a car (thus keeping Rafer happy) and drive to the University of California at Berkeley (fresh air for me). Tom had remembered one vital detail about Tina's family. Tina's father was Full-Blown Professor of Physics at UCB. We would find him and audit one of his lectures. Since José wanted to study, this simple plan made everyone happy. And High Pockets would enjoy lifting his leg on the trees and bushes.

I strolled casually around the building's parking lot, looking for suitable wheels. Almost everybody was at work, but a few drug dealers were still at home.* The problem was that most of these types have a lot of money and a lot of flash, so they prefer sports cars. There were four of us, so we needed a sedan, preferably a four-door (better for bolting from the vehicle). I finally found a Mercedes 280 SEL tucked away in a corner. Rafer's expertise in breaking-and-entering and hot-wiring landed him the job.

---

*A simple deduction: Almost all expensive cars that sit around all day (on weekdays) belong to drug dealers. A sign of the times, I suspect.

José was concerned about Tom's condition, but there was little we could do. The plan was to make him as comfortable as possible and call the paramedics as soon as we were safely out of the neighborhood. I taped a note to Tom's forehead suggesting that what Tom needed was not medical or psychiatric care, but a down-to-earth Subatomic Physicist who could give him some insight into the Underlying Nature of Reality, thereby putting Tom's problems in their proper perspective. I'm certain that someday this type of therapy will be commonplace. The teachings of Bohr, Lorenz and Planck will soon supplant the foolishness of Freud, Jung and Fromm. There is no doubt about it.

Sausalito Banditos
PART VII

The UCB physics department was a disappointment architecturally, having neither a Subatomic nor Macrocosmic look. It just looked like an old building. José didn't consider this important, and I supposed he's right, but I was hoping I'd have some kind of déjà vu experience when I got that close to a major seat of Subatomic Learning (not to mention Tina's father). Life is full of this sort of disappointment.

I left José, Rafer and High Pockets outside (instructing them to look casual) while I scouted the inside of the building. I was the only one of us who looked anything like a student, and I was slightly concerned that the Feds might've set up ambushes in all the Subatomic Hangouts in the area. The building looked clean, so I inquired about the lecture schedule. I was pleased to learn that Tina's father was, at that very moment, teaching a graduate course in Theoretical Physics at the main lecture hall.

The four of us entered the hall as unobtrusively as possible. Luckily it was a huge amphitheater and was only half full, so we were able to slip unnoticed into back row seats.

It was pretty dark in the back, but since José and I were nevertheless afraid that Tina's father might recognize him from the mugging in Colombia, José sat low in his seat and pulled the brim of his sombrero down over his eyes. I sat between Rafer and José, where I could do a running translation of the lecture for José and answer any simpleminded questions Rafer might have. High Pockets stretched out in the aisle and seemed to doze off.

Tina's father was a tall, lanky, big-boned man with distinguished gray hair. He was the epitome of the Subatomic Kind of Guy. You were sure he was going to light a pipe any second, then say something profound. I was in awe of the man. His lecture was full of insight and pregnant pauses. Rafer, God bless him, was dumbstruck. He sat quiet and wide-eyed as Tina's father probed beneath the Molecular to the Atomic, then, inevitably, to the Subatomic.

"And when we get to the subatomic level," Tina's father's voice echoed eerily, "what do we find? Nothing!"

Pregnant pause.

"Wee-oow," Rafer whispered.

"Ahhh," José responded to my translation. This was, of course, old hat for José and me, but hearing it from Tina's father made our neck hairs prickle.

"That's right. Nothing." His voice was very soft, very theatrical. "Subatomic particles are merely *concepts* constructed by the human mind to explain experience. They do not 'exist in reality' but are statistical *tendencies to exist* . . . . The problem for the physicist, among others, is that it is difficult if not impossible, to explain or predict their movements, their behavior. They are very disconcerting phenomena. To a classical physicist, their behavior is abominable. Unacceptable, even. Throw in a dose of Quantum Theory . . ."

A short, feral cry rose involuntarily from my throat at the mention of Quantum Theory, interrupting the lecture. Tina's father paused and squinted up in our direction. José slid further down in his seat. High Pockets woke up and started sneezing—easily the worst attack he'd ever had. His sneezes were short and very close together, three per second, I estimated, and very loud. Everyone in the hall turned to look back at us.

"Shit," I said. There is no known cure for High Pockets' attacks, so I usually just let them run their course, but this was an emergency. I threw myself over Rafer's legs and grabbed High Pockets' collar. With my other hand I covered his nose. He struggled and continued to sneeze, but nothing came out since I had plugged up his sneezing orifice. This apparently triggered some kind of doggy adrenaline reaction. He pulled me over Rafer, into the aisle, then proceeded to drag me down the stairs toward the podium.

My hand was caught under High Pockets' collar, so I let go of his nose and tried to free it. This released several horrendous sneezes (there had been a pressure buildup), forcing High Pockets to stop and steady himself. I wrenched my hand loose from his collar, but unfortunately lost my balance in the process. I fell over backward and continued to tumble down toward the podium. And Tina's father. This was upsetting. I didn't want our first meeting to be precipitated by Gravitational Theory, so I flailed my arms, searching for something to stop my descent. I found it in the form of someone's leg.

I thudded to a stop and looked around, dazed. The room began to spin. Someone nearby was screaming.

High Pockets was still sneezing.

I could hear José yelling in Spanish that we'd better go. At this point I must have lost consciousness because the next thing I remember is waking up in the backseat of our stolen Mercedes. We were doing well over a hundred miles per hour and police sirens were wailing everywhere.

Sausalito Banditos
PART VIII

Rafer led the cops on a wild chase through Berkeley, then headed north on a winding rural blacktop road. He dropped off the rest of us after executing a flawless four-wheel drift around a sharp curve. He said he'd lose the cops, steal another car and be back in time to get to our dinner engagement. We hid in the woods and waited.

He showed up at six-thirty with a new Coupe de Ville. Brand-new. He had nailed it right out of a showroom in downtown Berkeley. It was all scratched up from plowing through the front window of the dealership, but it was still an impressive heist. We celebrated his return by smoking several joints and drinking a considerable amount of tequila.

We hadn't eaten since we'd left Tom's, so the tequila and marijuana made us very high and very hungry. I hoped Tina's mother had the foresight to cook up extras. I hadn't mentioned anything about High Pockets or José, never mind Rafer. I'll tell you something about Rafer: That boy could flat *eat*.

At any rate, by seven o'clock we were good and fucked up and ready to cruise back over to Sausalito and get on with this crucial matter of Tina's father.

After a couple of tries we got off the freeway at the correct exit and commenced our search for Tina's father's house, which was on Birdbath Lane. As expected, Rafer's driving ability was severely affected by what we'd consumed in the woods. Birdbath Lane eluded him for quite some time.

It was a little after eight when we careened into their driveway and ran over a white Persian cat asleep on the pavement. Being animal lovers, José and I were upset by this development, but Rafer and High Pockets didn't even acknowledge the feline fatality. They were crazed with hunger and the smell of barbecuing steaks made them both grunt and whine. José wrapped the flattened Persian in one of his buckskin vests (he wore several layers) and put it aside for future burial.

I was trembling slightly when we reached the front porch, so I had a couple quick belts of tequila to calm my nerves. José was jumpy, too, which I'd never seen before. For some reason, his being nervous calmed me down a little.

"Open de goddamn door! We hungry!" Rafer called out, slurring badly. High Pockets offered one of his whines that turns into a bark.

"Ssshh!" I said.

"*Sí,*" José agreed. "*Silencio.*"

I took a deep breath and rang the doorbell three times.

Sausalito Banditos
PART IX

The door swung open. Tina's father squinted out at us, an unlit pipe in his mouth. (I knew it.) He blinked a few times at the sight of me and my motley crew of Bandito Truth Seekers. He seemed at a complete loss for words. I stared back in genuine shock: Electrons were circling Tina's father's head at near the speed of light. I wondered briefly whether anyone else noticed this phenomenon.

No one spoke for several seconds. I figured we were involved in some kind of weird Subatomic Standoff. Then it happened. He spoke. I searched his words for their Underlying Meaning, but I couldn't come up with anything. This is what he said:

"Can I help you?"

Eventually it occurred to me that there was no Underlying Meaning. He was just being polite. He was being . . . *civil*.

Here was this guy I had been sending weird messages to, potentially Worldview-shattering messages (remember what happened to Tom and Gary), for months. He had answered me, *encouraged* me, asked me to dinner, for God's sake, through clandestine ads in the *International Trib* and the *San Francisco Chronicle*.

I had risked life and limb in a death-defying trek through war-torn Bandito Strongholds and predator-infested jungles to confront this man, to probe his intellect for a clue or even a vague metaphor that might assuage my torn and bleeding vision of What It All Means. Tina's father was staring at a severely angst-ridden guy and all he could come up with was "Can I help you?"

"Fucking-A Right you can!" I roared.

Sausalito Banditos

PART X

There was a mad scramble. Tina's father slammed the door and bolted it before we could drive through. I was slightly dazed. Things were not working out as I had planned.

Subatomic Particles were zipping through the Continuum all around me, some colliding with others to form new and more colorful Subatomic Particles. Some released energy, others absorbed it. I briefly sensed a kind of balance. They were, I knew, obeying some Subatomic Code of Conduct beyond the scope of human understanding. A Code of Conduct that transcended the absurd moralistic and logic-ridden human Worldview. A Code of Conduct that *incorporated* randomness and chaos into an intrinsically paradoxical nonphilosophy. Their ability to approach the speed of light and thereby tinker with time travel made me fleetingly envious.

I looked at José. I could see a Bandito Temper Flare-Up coming on so I dove for cover, yelling to Rafer and High Pockets to do the same.

"*Ai-ee-ah!*" This was José's Bandito Yell, which he reserved for those occasions that required superhuman strength or courage.

José went through the door like an X ray through molybdenum. The bolt disintegrated and one hinge flew off. Rafer, High Pockets and I entered. José put the door back into its frame and followed us into the living room.

Next to Tina's father, Tina and Tina's mother were standing together, looking very much alike. Tina's father didn't look as Subatomic as he had when lecturing earlier at UCB. He just looked scared.

When Tina's mother saw José she fainted on the spot.* Tina screamed, then picked up a large glass ashtray and hurled it at me, which was pretty insightful. She somehow sensed that I had been responsible for exposing, as it were, her Nympho-maniacal Worldview. When I ducked the airborne ashtray, she snatched some other knickknack with more violent intentions, but Rafer grabbed and subdued her. She was so crazed with pent-up anger and sexual frustration that Rafer was forced to bind and gag her.**

Rafer and High Pockets then bolted for the kitchen, where it soon sounded like feeding time at the zoo. José put his .45 to Tina's father's head and guided him to the dining room table, where he motioned for him to sit. José placed his piece on the table, then put a dent in our last bottle of tequila and offered Tina's father a belt. The man was too petrified to respond.

I sat across from him and stared at the electrons buzzing around his head like busy little Subatomic Bees.

"I'm Mr. Quark," I said.

"I have money," he said breathlessly. "Please don't hurt my family."

"I am Mr. Quark," I repeated patiently. "My associates and I are here by your invitation."

"There—there must be some mistake."

"There's no mistake."

I extracted a wad of paper from my pants pocket and began to sort it out. One by one I placed the classified ads he'd written in front of him.

"Uh. I . . . I don't know . . . anything about these," he said.

---

*Since the mugging she had apparently been plagued with recurring Bandito Nightmares.
**As it turned out, Tina had been permanently grounded and her new dia-phragm confiscated by her father after Gary called one night, roaring drunk, from the Crisco Disco West and spilled the sexual beans.

José wanted to know what was going on. As I filled him in, Rafer and High Pockets came in from the kitchen, both with steak bones in their mouths. Rafer had a handful of salad in one hand and a fresh steak in the other. He addressed Tina's father. " 'Killya. Mo' 'killya."

"Oh, God . . . Please don't kill me," he begged, but my mind was elsewhere and racing.

"What happened to my messages?" I demanded, trying to ignore the spectacular Subatomic Particle Display that had erupted all around.

"Wait a minute," Tina's father said, having just had an "A-ha!" experience. "Are you the lunatic from South America?" He blanched in fear. "I mean, uh, the *person* from South America?"

"Yes," I said. "I am."

I was starting to feel nauseous. Something was seriously amiss here.

"I put an ad in the *International Herald Tribune* months ago, as you instructed. I asked you to leave me and my family alone."

He was saying this as if it would calm me down. All it did, as a matter of fact, was increase the intensity of the Subatomic Particle Bombardment I was experiencing. He continued his devastating tirade. "I instructed the post office not to deliver any more letters with South American stamps on them. They were upsetting my wife. It's been at least six months since I received any, uh, messages.* I'm sorry if—"

"Quiet, please," I mumbled. "I have to think." I was perspiring freely now.

"Mo' 'killya," Rafer wheezed, then had a belt from the bottle on the table.

"*Que pasó?*" José inquired. I told him what had happened.

---

*In one fell swoop, Tina's father had invalidated both the Simultaneous Bandito Stronghold Theory and the Concept of the Creeping Banditos.

His face turned white. I'd never seen this before either. Then I noticed something else: Electrons were circling José's head as well as Tina's father's. One electron jumped from Tina's father's head to José's. In theory, this would change the elemental properties of both their heads, but I was unable to pursue this train of thought any further. These new developments were too upsetting.

In desperation I addressed Rafer, hoping he would come up with something I could relate to. "If Tina's father didn't write those ads, who did?"

The answer came in the form of a wild pounding on the front door.

José cocked his piece.

High Pockets growled.

Tina's father whimpered.

Rafer said, "Wee-oow."

I was struck by several million Subatomic Particles.

The front door burst open, then fell off its remaining hinge and crashed to the floor.

Jim, Robert, Flash and Aileron staggered in. They were about as fucked up as I'd ever seen them.

Sausalito Banditos

PART XI

High Pockets and Aileron enjoyed another doggy reunion. José was so surprised and pleased that he forgot all about Tina's father. He rushed into the living room, letting loose his second Bandito Yell of the evening.

Tina's mother briefly regained consciousness, took a good look at her new guests, then returned to la-la land.

Tina was giving me the evil eye from the couch. I was glad she was tied up. Someday I would have to explain all this to her.

Rafer, God bless him, had passed out, his head resting on the dining room table, his hand outstretched toward the tequila.

Tina's father was hyperventilating. He had failed miserably when it came to putting anything in its proper perspective. I would do better, I promised myself.

I squinted through the Subatomic Particle Shower toward the living room. I was too disoriented to react to the sudden appearance of Jim, Robert, Flash and Aileron. I did sense, however, that another bombshell was about to be dropped.

I looked at Robert. The first thing I noticed was that he was wearing a tuxedo. This I hadn't seen before. He had a grenade in one hand and a bottle of Grand Marnier in the other. He had lost his faculty of coherent speech but was attempting to carry on a conversation with José anyway.

Flash was romping with High Pockets and Aileron. I couldn't tell what he or Jim were wearing because of the amount and nature of the stains and holes in their clothes. Jim was approaching me through the multicolored Subatomic Haze. Smiling from behind a vibrating Electron Aura, he sat down across from me.

"Hi, Sport," he said, "or should I call you 'Mr. Quark?' "

"It was you guys all the time," I managed to say.

"We found your shack a week or so after you and José left. From the notes and stuff you left around, we figured you were heading here. That was sloppy, leaving that stuff lying around. Excuse me."

Jim bent over and threw up on the floor. He looked at Tina's father and shrugged. "Anyway, we flew up here and bribed the postal authorities to give us any mail with grease-ball stamps on it. Then we zipped down to Mexico and tracked you maniacs down by air by using the postmarks as your trail."

"A Beech-18," I croaked.

"Right. José nearly shot us down with his fucking Thompson."

I could feel the bedrock of my Worldview crumbling beneath me.

"We knew that if all else failed, we could always intercept you loonies at this address. We sort of *guided* you here with the ads in the *Trib*."

I let out a groan. A Subatomic Groan if ever there was one.

"What was all that garbage about the underlying, ah, whatever of reality?"

"Garbage," I repeated mindlessly.

"We couldn't let you and ol' José go off the deep end like that, buddy. You guys are our brothers."

"*Flapgolbadwok!*" Robert yelled from the living room. He had whipped out a couple more grenades and was doing his juggling routine. José was chug-a-lugging Robert's Grand Marnier.

I found myself staring at a fruit bowl in the middle of Tina's family's dining room table. There were two apples in there, along with an orange, a peach and a radioactive banana. I tried to remember what the half-life of a radioactive banana was, but my memory failed me.

I then thought briefly of the old Indian, Señor Rodriguez, Colonel Menendez, and Tom and Gary. I glanced at Rafer, God bless him, then at Tina, Tina's mother and, finally, Tina's father. I wondered where Tina's sister, Ruth, was and if she was always left out when it came to family gatherings. The thought crossed my mind that, in the final analysis, Ruth was probably at the bottom of all this.

I felt very alone.

Jim jerked his thumb in the direction of Tina's father. "And who the fuck is *this* dude?" Jim shook his head. "We're gonna have to straighten you guys out, me and Robert."

Jim dumped a few grams of coke on the table and flicked open a switchblade. He started chopping, then tossed me a thick, pungent joint. "Fire that sucker up," he said.

Flash was chasing High Pockets and Aileron around the living room.

Tina was staring at me malevolently. I had to look away. Whatever she was thinking, she was probably right.

Rafer was still passed out. He started to snore.

Tina's father was staring at Jim, his eyes pleading. I was completely disillusioned with the man. Even the electrons had abandoned him.

"*Grantalaraw!*" Robert yelled and threw something into the kitchen.

José staggered into the dining room, fell onto the table and passed out.

"At least José's coming to his senses," Jim said. "You're next."

As it turned out, it was a live grenade that Robert had thrown into the kitchen. At this point it went off. I was struck by flying debris and lost consciousness.

Epilogue

I feel that I have some explaining to do.

As I already mentioned, two months or so have elapsed since the Sausalito escapade and I have only recently recovered from the mental trauma that resulted. Though I've managed to put quite a few things in their proper perspective, I still have a ways to go.

I am writing these words from the veranda of our villa in Riohacha, Colombia. The view is spectacular and we are all ridiculously wealthy again.*

I am still a student of the cosmos, but the conclusions I was forced to come to that night in Sausalito have taken the wind out of my subatomic sails. (Notice that I don't capitalize "subatomic" anymore.) I had taken everything much too seriously

---

*This is the other end of the Time Travel Footnote on page 71, where I explained that the old Indian had gone back on his fast. At that time I was contacting you from the future, which is now. And it was yesterday that I visited the old Indian in his cave up in the mountains.

and was therefore devastated to find out that I was a clown in a larger, less comprehensible circus. It had been the height of arrogance for me to consider myself the ringmaster of anything. I suspect that as the circuses get bigger (or smaller), they become less and less comprehensible and probably goofier and goofier until only God gets the joke. Trying to comprehend the underlying nature of reality is an example of this in one direction, and trying to comprehend man's place in the universe is an example in the other direction. I don't try to do either of these things anymore, but I enjoy discussing them because it makes me feel intelligent.

As a result of this attitude, I have ceased feeling foolish about being a clown. One thing that amuses me about most people is that they resent the idea that they're clowns.

The life I lived prior to becoming obsessed with the new physics is an example of a life that was in tune with this circus atmosphere that makes up the human condition. This is the wisdom of Robert and Jim. They are true Zen clowns. I have proof of this. Here it is: If I try to explain any of this to them, they laugh at me.

The essence of wisdom is probably not to think about it. Rafer, God bless him, has always known this. He's here with us in Riohacha, by the way, and is also ridiculously wealthy. He has proven to be an invaluable asset in planning our criminal activities, and he is also a master at putting things in their proper perspective. When things don't go exactly as we plan, he smiles stoically and says, "Wee-oow."

José says, "Ahh."

I usually say something like, "Shit ass rat fuck." I have a lot of catching up to do.

I should probably explain how we all got back here to Riohacha and became ridiculously wealthy again. I'll just give you the basic facts. Here they are:

Jim and Robert didn't spend night one in jail after being overrun by federal agents in Miami. Robert had been holding a serious trump card for years and chose to play it at that time. It had to do with some documents and tapes he had swiped from the State Department when he was working for Nixon and his gang of creeps. He had stashed copies of the material in various safe deposit boxes, which were to be opened upon Robert's death or incarceration. Everyone in Washington nowadays is very concerned about Robert's health and well-being.

As I more or less suspected, it was Robert and Jim who had informed the authorities about my imaginary terrorist activities, inadvertently causing José to have his Colombian Empire pillaged by a malicious Rival Dope Lord. They had done this as a joke, of course, not foreseeing any ramifications down the line. As the astute reader will already have sensed, this mindless prank was a crucial domino in a chain reaction that led to uncountable weird occurrences in the lives of uncountable people. José's mugging of Tina's family, and all of *its* ramifications, (possibly an infinite number of them) is only one example.* I tend to reflect back on this whenever I have the audacity to think that I have anything to say about anything.

Anyway, Robert demanded the return of our Learjet and split the $890,000 we had in the back with the agents who had apprehended Jim and him. This is standard procedure, and neither the cops nor the crooks consider this sort of thing a bribe. It is more a reward for a game well played.

Robert and Jim then spent a few days partying with the Feds and Eduardo in Miami. After going through most of the remaining cash, they hightailed it for the Cayman Islands, where they managed to remember what bank our two million

---

*José would never have bothered to mug anybody if he hadn't been stripped of his fortune. (This footnote is aimed at the unastute reader.)

was stashed in. After making the withdrawal, they began searching for José and me. It ended, of course, on that awful night in Sausalito.

After Robert blew up Tina's family's house (for some reason, no one was seriously injured), we made good our escape from Sausalito and found Harry and the Lear waiting at an airport in nearby Novato. (I was still unconscious, so this information is secondhand.)

We then flew to New York and looked up George again. George had moved to another warehouse, but it was business as usual. And we were lucky. He was having a special on Mac-10 machine pistols, AK-47s and all rocket launchers. We bought nearly a million dollars' worth of armament and began planning an all-out Bandito Assault on Riohacha in order to re-capture José's Empire and return him to his rightful position of Full-Blown Dope Lord.

Meanwhile, Flash and Aileron had flown down to the Ba-hamas to pick up the DC-4 the boys had bought for transport-ing whatever merch needed transporting.

As it turned out, recapturing José's Empire was a piece of cake. His rival had turned out to be a Creepy Dope Lord. Everyone in Riohacha missed José, who was widely considered a Mellow Dope Lord. We raised an army of several hundred Guajiran Indians and Disgruntled Banditos and marched into Riohacha unopposed. The Creepy Dope Lord ran like a thief and has not been heard from since.

Flash and Aileron made several successful runs for us in the DC-4, and I became Admiral of our own little Marijuana Navy.

Things have more or less returned to abnormal. José and I hold informal seminars on the new physics for those Banditos who care to attend, but as I said, we don't take it so seriously anymore. It's better to simply *live* a subatomic sort of lifestyle than to go off half-cocked about it and not get anything done.

This, it seems to me, is the problem with most so-called philosophers. They never get anything *done.*

I sent a substantial amount of money to Tina's father to cover the cost of rebuilding their house and to pay for psychiatric care for Tina's mother. By coincidence, Tina's mother now occupies a room that adjoins Tom's in a private mental hospital in Marin County. I know this because I am footing Tom's bill also. Nobody in Tina's family knows anything about Tom being in the hospital or how he got there.

I dropped poor Gary a note explaining everything and apologizing for any inconvenience I may have caused him. I told him that if there were ever any psychiatric or medical repercussions of my visit to San Francisco, he should put an ad in the *International Herald Tribune* addressed to "Mr. Quark" (why not?), giving the name of the doctor or hospital and the amount of the bill, and I would cover it. I then said that José sends his love (a lie, of course) and signed off.*

If the reader finds it incredible (and possibly immoral) that this tale has a happy ending, he is not the only one. I, too, am astounded. For those who feel that my associates' and my criminal antics are a perversion of everything that is right and good, take heart. There is an excellent chance that I will come to a ghastly end. (I suspect that my demise will have something to do with Robert and his interest in high explosives.) But for the reader or me to become obsessed with this probability would mean that we have missed something somewhere along the way, although I have no idea what.

I should probably mention that I do not know specifically what the message here is, if indeed there is one. If anyone out

---

*About two weeks after I sent Gary this note, an ad addressed to "Mr. Quark" *did* appear in the *International Herald Trib.* The body of the message was unintelligible, however.

there has a theory, please contact José and me through the *International Trib* in the prescribed way. We would be interested in hearing from you.

When all is said and done, when all the shouting and philosophizing and moralizing is over, I suspect that this tale is simply another example of something.

The attempt to understand the universe is one of the only things that elevates the human condition from farce to the elegance of tragedy.
—Stephen Weinberg, Nobel Laureate in Physics, 1979

Author's Note

As mentioned in the Foreword to the New Edition, I recently spent two years in Central America. Assuming you were paying attention, you will also remember that I was down there looking for an old friend and sometime partner in crime who had disappeared a few years previously. And that while I was searching for him and wandering around, a lot of stuff happened.

I've written a book about it all: the search, the stuff, my shamelessly misspent younger years, you name it.* *In Search of Captain Zero* is the title. Although the word *memoir* appears nowhere in or on the book, that's essentially what it is.

It's about as different from this book as it's possible to be.**

I bring this up in case you didn't like this book. See, if you

---

*A careful reading will also reveal which incidents in this current book were inspired by real events in my life.
**It has only one footnote, for example.

didn't like this book, you're virtually guaranteed to like *In Search of Captain Zero*. They're that different.

But: If you *did* like this book, you're also virtually guaranteed to like *In Search of Captain Zero*. Never mind if this doesn't sound quite right. Just trust me on it.

For proof of how different *In Search of Captain Zero* is from this book, or possibly any other book you've ever read, you can visit my Web site, *www.aweisbecker.com*.* A guided tour, with lots of photos, awaits you.

You'll also find that *this* book is shamelessly touted on my Web site. I've even reproduced the Foreword to the New Edition there, which, presumably, you've already read.

You may want to read it again, just to make sure.**

---

*Yes, I've come a long way for a guy who thought Amazon.com was a wilderness outfitter.

**You may also want to buy lots of copies of both books, which you can do through Amazon.com or my own Web site. Listen: In the Foreword to the New Edition I claim that I've gotten no advance from the publisher on this book. *I wasn't kidding.* Zip. And you wouldn't believe how little I get in terms of per copy royalties. *Less than a buck.* (Where's all that money going? A bunch of jerks in suits, where else?) But if you buy a few books, maybe I can make ends meet. I'm counting on you.(!)

(!) This is a Footnote To A Footnote (FTAF—pronounced "Fitaff"), which is something I've been dying to pull off. It occurs to me that, given the astronomical rise in value of copies of the last edition, you may want to buy hundreds or even thousands of copies of this edition. As part of your retirement plan, say.

ABOUT THE AUTHOR

Not much is known about A.C. Weisbecker
and A.C. Weisbecker wants to keep it that way.*

---

*I know: This doesn't work anymore. The phrase *the cat's out of the bag* comes
to mind.